MW01503757

FICTION

Prayer
by Robert Reed

Synch Me, Kiss Me, Drop
by Suzanne Church

All the Things the Moon is Not
by Alexander Lumans

NON-FICTION

The Fairy Tale in the TV Age
by Alethea Kontis

Straightforward and Unadorned Adventure:
A Conversation with Michael J. Sullivan
by Jeremy L. C. Jones

Another Word:
Dear Speculative Fiction, I'm Glad We Had this Talk
by Elizabeth Bear

From the Editor's Desk
by Neil Clarke

Sci-fi Farmer (Cover Art)
by Jessada Sutthi

Prayer
ROBERT REED

Fashion matters. In my soul of souls, I know that the dead things you carry on your body are real, real important. Grandma likes to call me a clotheshorse, which sounds like a good thing. For example, I've always known that a quality sweater means the world. I prefer soft organic wools woven around Class-C nanofibers—a nice high collar with sleeves riding a little big but with enough stopping power to absorb back-to-back kinetic charges. I want pants that won't slice when the shrapnel is thick, and since I won't live past nineteen, probably, I let the world see that this body's young and fit. (Morbid maybe, but that's why I think about death only in little doses.) I adore elegant black boots that ignore rain and wandering electrical currents, and everything under my boots and sweater and pants has to feel silky-good against the most important skin in my world. But essential beyond all else is what I wear on my face, which is more makeup than Grandma likes, and tattooed scripture on the forehead, and sparkle-eyes that look nothing but ordinary. In other words, I want people to see an average Christian girl instead of what I am, which is part of the insurgency's heart inside Occupied Toronto.

To me, guns are just another layer of clothes, and the best day ever lived was the day I got my hands on a barely-used, cognitively damaged Mormon railgun. They don't make that model anymore, what with its willingness to change sides. And I doubt that there's ever been a more dangerous gun made by the human species. Shit, the boy grows his own ammo, and he can kill anything for hundreds of miles, and left alone he will invent ways to hide and charge himself on the sly, and all that time he waits waits waits for his master to come back around and hold him again.

I am his master now.

1

I am Ophelia Hanna Hanks, except within my local cell, where I wear the randomly generated, perfectly suitable name:

Ridiculous.

The gun's name is Prophet, and until ten seconds ago, he looked like scrap conduit and junk wiring. And while he might be cognitively impaired, Prophet is wickedly loyal to me. Ten days might pass without the two of us being in each other's reach, but that's the beauty of our dynamic: I can live normal and look normal, and while the enemy is busy watching everything else, a solitary fourteen-year-old girl slips into an alleyway that's already been swept fifty times today.

"Good day, Ridiculous."

"Good day to you, Prophet."

"And who are we going to drop into Hell today?"

"All of America," I say, which is what I always say.

Reliable as can be, he warns me, "That's a rather substantial target, my dear. Perhaps we should reduce our parameters."

"Okay. New Fucking York."

Our attack has a timetable, and I have eleven minutes to get into position.

"And the specific target?" he asks.

I have coordinates that are updated every half-second. I could feed one or two important faces into his menu, but I never kill faces. These are the enemy, but if I don't define things too closely, then I won't miss any sleep tonight.

Prophet eats the numbers, saying, "As you wish, my dear."

I'm carrying him, walking fast towards a fire door that will stay unlocked for the next ten seconds. Alarmed by my presence, a skinny rat jumps out of one dumpster, little legs running before it hits the oily bricks.

"Do you know it?" I ask.

The enemy likes to use rats as spies.

Prophet says, "I recognize her, yes. She has a nest and pups inside the wall."

"Okay," I say, feeling nervous and good.

The fire door opens when I tug and locks forever once I step into the darkness.

"You made it," says my gun.

"I was praying," I report.

He laughs, and I laugh too. But I keep my voice down, stairs needing to be climbed and only one of us doing the work.

• • •

She found me after a battle. She believes that I am a little bit stupid. I was damaged in the fight and she imprinted my devotions to her, and then using proxy tools and stolen wetware, she gave me the cognitive functions to be a loyal agent to the insurgency.

I am an astonishing instrument of mayhem, and naturally her superiors thought about claiming me for themselves.

But they didn't.

If I had the freedom to speak, I would mention this oddity to my Ridiculous. "Why would they leave such a prize with little you?"

"Because I found you first," she would say.

"War isn't a schoolyard game," I'd remind her.

"But I made you mine," she might reply. "And my bosses know that I'm a good soldier, and you like me, and stop being a turd."

No, we have one another because her bosses are adults. They are grown souls who have survived seven years of occupation, and that kind of achievement doesn't bless the dumb or the lucky. Looking at me, they see too much of a blessing, and nobody else dares to trust me well enough to hold me.

I know all of this, which seems curious.

I might say all of this, except I never do.

And even though my mind was supposedly mangled, I still remember being crafted and calibrated in Utah, hence my surname. But I am no Mormon. Indeed, I'm a rather agnostic soul when it comes to my interpretations of Jesus and His influence in the New World. And while there are all-Mormon units in the US military, I began my service with Protestants—Baptists and Missouri Synods mostly. They were bright clean happy believers who had recently arrived at Fort Joshua out on Lake Ontario. Half of that unit had already served a tour in Alberta, guarding the tar pits from little acts of sabotage. Keeping the Keystones safe is a critical but relatively simple duty. There aren't many people to watch, just robots and one another. The prairie was depopulated ten years ago, which wasn't an easy or cheap process; American farmers still haven't brought the ground back to full production, and that's one reason why the Toronto rations are staying small.

But patrolling the corn was easy work compared to sitting inside Fort Joshua, millions of displaced and hungry people staring at your walls.

Americans call this Missionary Work.

Inside their own quarters, alone except for their weapons and the Almighty, soldiers try to convince one another that the natives are beginning to love them. Despite a thousand lessons to the contrary, Canada is still that baby brother to the north, big and foolish but congenial in his heart, or at least capable of learning manners after the loving sibling delivers enough beat-downs.

What I know today—what every one of my memories tells me—is that the American soldiers were grossly unprepared. Compared to other units and other duties, I would even go so far as to propose that the distant generals were aware of their limitations yet sent the troops across the lake regardless, full of religion and love for each other and the fervent conviction that the United States was the empire that the world had always deserved.

Canada is luckier than most. That can't be debated without being deeply, madly stupid. Heat waves are killing the tropics. Acid has tortured the seas. The wealth of the previous centuries has been erased by disasters of weather and war and other inevitable surprises. But the worst of these sorrows haven't occurred in the Greater United States, and if they had half a mind, Canadians would be thrilled with the mild winters and long brilliant summers and the supportive grip of their big wise master.

My soldiers' first recon duty was simple: Walk past the shops along Queen.

Like scared warriors everywhere, they put on every piece of armor and every sensor and wired back-ups that would pierce the insurgent's jamming. And that should have been good enough. But by plan or by accident, some native let loose a few molecules of VX gas—just enough to trigger one of the biohazard alarms. Then one of my brother-guns was leveled at a crowd of innocents, two dozen dead before the bloody rain stopped flying.

That's when the firefight really began.

Kinetic guns and homemade bombs struck the missionaries from every side. I was held tight by my owner—a sergeant with commendations for his successful defense of a leaky pipeline—but he didn't fire me once. His time was spent yelling for an orderly retreat, pleading with his youngsters to find sure targets before they hit the buildings with hypersonic rounds. But despite those good smart words, the patrol got itself trapped. There was a genuine chance that one of them might die, and that's what those devout men encased in body armor and faith decided to pray: Clasping hands, they opened channels to the Almighty, begging for thunder to be sent down on the infidels.

The Almighty is what used to be called the Internet—an American child reclaimed totally back in 2027.

A long stretch of shops and old buildings was struck from the sky.

That's what American soldiers do when the situation gets dicey. They pray, and the locals die by the hundreds, and the biggest oddity of that

4

peculiar day was how the usual precise orbital weaponry lost its way, and half of my young men were wounded or killed in the onslaught while a tiny shaped charge tossed me a hundred meters down the road.

There I was discovered in the rubble by a young girl.

As deeply unlikely as that seems.

I don't want the roof. I don't need my eyes to shoot. An abandoned apartment on the top floor is waiting for me, and in particular, its dirty old bathroom. As a rule, I like bathrooms. They're the strongest part of any building, what with pipes running through the walls and floor. Two weeks ago, somebody I'll never know sealed the tube's drain and cracked the faucet just enough for a slow drip, and now the water sits near the brim. Water is essential for long shots. With four minutes to spare, I deploy Prophet's long legs, tipping him just enough toward the southeast, and then I sink him halfway into the bath, asking, "How's that feel?"

"Cold," he jokes.

We have three and a half minutes to talk.

I tell him, "Thank you."

His barrel stretches to full length, its tip just short of the moldy plaster ceiling. "Thank you for what?" he says.

"I don't know," I say.

Then I laugh, and he sort of laughs.

I say, "I'm not religious. At least, I don't want to be."

"What are you telling me, Ridiculous?"

"I guess . . . I don't know. Forget it."

And he says, "I will do my very best."

Under the water, down where the breech sits, ammunition is moving. Scrap metal and scrap nano-fibers have been woven into four bullets. Street fights require hundreds and thousands of tiny bullets, but each of these rounds is bigger than most carrots and shaped the same general way. Each one carries a brain and microrockets and eyes. Prophet is programming them with the latest coordinates while running every last-second test. Any little problem with a bullet can mean an ugly shot, or even worse, an explosion that rips away the top couple floors of this building.

At two minutes, I ask, "Are we set?"

"You're standing too close," he says.

"If I don't move, will you fire anyway?"

"Of course."

"Good," I say.

At ninety-five seconds, ten assaults are launched across southern Ontario. The biggest and nearest is fixated on Fort Joshua—homemade cruise missiles and lesser railguns aimed at that artificial island squatting in our beautiful lake. The assaults are meant to be loud and unexpected, and because every soldier thinks his story is important, plenty of voices suddenly beg with the Almighty, wanting His godly hand.

The nearby battle sounds like a sudden spring wind.

"I'm backing out of here," I say.

"Please do," he says.

At sixty-one seconds, most of the available American resources are glancing at each of these distractions, and a brigade of AIs is studying past tendencies and elaborate models of insurgency capabilities, coming to the conclusion that these events have no credible value toward the war's successful execution.

Something else is looming, plainly.

"God's will," says the nonbeliever.

"What isn't?" says the Mormon gun.

At seventeen seconds, two kilometers of the Keystone John pipeline erupt in a line of smoky flame, microbombs inside the heated tar doing their best to stop the flow of poisons to the south.

The Almighty doesn't need prayer to guide His mighty hand. This must be the main attack, and every resource is pulled to the west, making ready to deal with even greater hazards.

I shut the bathroom door and run for the hallway.

Prophet empties his breech, the first carrot already moving many times faster than the speed of sound as it blasts through the roof. Its three buddies are directly behind it, and the enormous release of stored energy turns the bathwater to steam, and with the first shot the iron tub is yanked free of the floor while the second and third shots kick the tub and the last of its water down into the bathroom directly downstairs. The final shot is going into the wrong part of the sky, but that's also part of the plan. I'm not supposed to be amazed by how many factors can be juggled at once, but they are juggled and I am amazed, running down the stairs to recover my good friend.

The schedule is meant to be secret and followed precisely. The Secretary of Carbon rides her private subway car to the UN, but instead of remaining indoors and safe, she has to come into the sunshine, standing with ministers and potentates who have gathered for this very important conference. Reporters are sitting in rows and cameras will be watching from every vantage point, and both groups are full of those who don't particularly like the Secretary. Part of her job is being despised, and fuck them. That's what she thinks whenever she attends these big public dances. Journalists are livestock, and this is a show put on for the meat. Yet even as the scorn builds, she shows a smile that looks warm and caring, and she carries a strong speech that will last for three minutes, provided she gives it. Her words are meant to reassure the world that full recovery is at hand. She will tell everyone that the hands of her government are wise and what the United States wants is happiness for every living breathing wonderful life on this great world—a world that with God's help will live for another five billion years.

For the camera, for the world, the Secretary of Carbon and her various associates invest a few moments in handshakes and important nods of the head.

Watching from a distance, without knowing anything, it would be easy to recognize that the smiling woman in brown was the one in charge.

The UN president shakes her hand last and then steps up to the podium. He was installed last year after an exhaustive search. Handsome and personable, and half as bright as he is ambitious, the President greets the press and then breaks from the script, shouting a bland "Hello" to the protestors standing outside the blast screens.

Five thousand people are standing in the public plaza, holding up signs and generated holos that have one clear message:

"END THE WARS NOW."

The Secretary knows the time and the schedule, and she feels a rare ache of nervousness, of doubt.

When they hear themselves mentioned, the self-absorbed protestors join together in one rehearsed shout that carries across the screens. A few reporters look at the throng behind them. The cameras and the real professionals focus on the human subjects. This is routine work. Reflexes are numb, minds lethargic. The Secretary picks out a few familiar faces, and then her assistant pipes a warning into her sparkle-eyes. One of the Keystones has been set on fire.

In reflex, the woman takes one step backward, her hands starting to lift to cover her head.

A mistake.

But she recovers soon enough, turning to her counterpart from Russia, telling him, "And congratulations on that new daughter of yours."

He is flustered and flattered. With a giddy nod, he says, "Girls are so much better than boys these days. Don't you think?"

The Secretary has no chance to respond.

A hypersonic round slams through the atmosphere, heated to a point where any impact will make it explode. Then it drops into an environment

7

*full of clutter and one valid target that must be acquired and reached
before the fabulous energies shake loose from their bridle.*

There is no warning sound.

*The explosion lifts bodies and pieces of bodies, and while the debris
rises, three more rounds plunge into the panicked crowd.*

Every person in the area drops flat, hands over their heads.

*Cameras turn, recording the violence and loss—more than three
hundred dead and maimed in a horrific attack.*

The Secretary and new father lie together on the temporary stage.

Is it her imagination, or is the man trying to cop a feel?

*She rolls away from him, but she doesn't stand yet. The attack is finished,
but she shouldn't know that. It's best to remain down and act scared, looking
at the plaza, the air filled with smoke and pulverized concrete while the
stubborn holos continue to beg for some impossible gift called Peace.*

My grandmother is sharp. She is. Look at her once in the wrong way,
and she knows something is wrong. Do it twice and she'll probably
piece together what makes a girl turn quiet and strange.

But not today, she doesn't.

"What happened at school?" she asks.

I don't answer.

"What are you watching, Ophelia?"

Nothing. My eyes have been blank for half a minute now.

"Something went wrong at school, didn't it?"

Nothing is ever a hundred percent right at school, which is why
it's easy to harvest a story that might be believed. Most people would
believe it, at least. But after listening to my noise about snippy friends
and broken trusts, she says, "I don't know what's wrong with you, honey.
But that isn't it."

I nod, letting my voice die away.

She leaves my little room without closing the door. I sit and do nothing
for about three seconds, and then the sparkle eyes take me back to the
mess outside the UN. I can't count the times I've watched the impacts,
the carnage. Hundreds of cameras were working, government cameras
and media cameras and those carried by the protesters. Following at the
digitals' heels are people talking about the tragedy and death tolls and
who is responsible and how the war has moved to a new awful level.

"Where did the insurgents get a top-drawer railgun?" faces ask.

But I've carried Prophet for a couple years and fired him plenty of
times. Just not into a public target like this, and with so many casualties,
and all of the dead on my side of the fight.

8

That's the difference here: The world suddenly knows about me.

In the middle of the slaughter, one robot camera stays focused on my real targets, including the Secretary of Fuel and Bullshit. It's halfway nice, watching her hunker down in terror. Except she should have been in pieces, and there shouldn't be a face staring in my direction, and how Prophet missed our target by more than fifty meters is one big awful mystery that needs solving.

I assume a malfunction.

I'm wondering where I can take him to get his guidance systems recalibrated and ready for retribution.

Unless of course the enemy has figured out how to make railgun rounds fall just a little wide of their goals, maybe even killing some troublemakers in the process.

Whatever is wrong here, at least I know that it isn't my fault.

Then some little thing taps at my window.

From the next room, my grandmother asks, "What are you doing, Ophelia?"

I'm looking at the bird on my window sill. The enemy uses rats, and we use robins and house sparrows. But this is a red-headed woodpecker, which implies rank and special circumstances.

The bird gives a squawk, which is a coded message that my eyes have to play with for a little while. Then the messenger flies away.

"Ophelia?"

"I'm just thinking about a friend," I shout.

She comes back into my room, watching my expression all over again.

"A friend, you say?"

"He's in trouble," I say.

"Is that what's wrong?" she asks.

"Isn't that enough?"

Two rats in this alley don't convince me. I'm watching them from my new haven, measuring the dangers and possible responses. Then someone approaches the three of us, and in the best tradition of ratdom, my companions scurry into the darkness under a pile of rotting boards.

I am a plastic sack filled with broken machine parts.

I am motionless and harmless, but in my secret reaches, inside my very busy mind, I'm astonished to see my Ridiculous back again so soon, walking toward the rat-rich wood pile.

Five meters behind her walks an unfamiliar man.

To him, I take an immediate dislike.

He looks prosperous, and he looks exceptionally angry, wearing a fine suit made stiff with nano-armor and good leather shoes and a platoon of jamming equipment as well as two guns riding in his pockets, one that shoots poisoned ice as well as the gun that he trusts—a kinetic beast riding close to his dominate hand.

Ridiculous stops at the rot pile.

The man asks, "Is it there?"

"I don't know," she says, eyes down.

My girl has blue sparkle eyes, much like her original eyes—the ones left behind in the doctor's garbage bin.

"It looks like boards now?" he asks.

"He did," she lies.

"Not he," the man says, sounding like a google-head. "The machine is an It."

"Right," she says, kicking at the planks, pretending to look hard. "It's just a big gun. I keep forgetting."

The man is good at being angry. He has a tall frightful face and neck muscles that can't stop being busy. His right hand thinks about the gun in his pocket. The fingers keep flexing, wanting to grab it.

His gun is an It.

I am not.

"I put it here," she says.

She put me where I am now, which tells me even more.

"Something scared it," she says. "And now it's moved to another hiding place."

The man says, "Shit."

Slowly, carefully, he turns in a circle, looking at the rubble and the trash and the occasional normal object that might still work or might be me. Then with a tight slow voice, he says, "Call for it."

"Prophet," she says.

I say nothing.

"How far could it move?" he asks.

"Not very," she says. "The firing drained it down to nothing, nearly. And it hasn't had time to feed itself, even if it's found food."

"Bullshit," he says, coming my way.

Ridiculous watches me and him, the tattooed Scripture above her blue eyes dripping with sweat. Then the man kneels beside me, and she says, "I put the right guidance codes into him."

"You said that already." Then he looks back at her, saying, "You're not in trouble here. I told you that already."

His voice says a lot.

I have no power. But when his hands reach into my sack, what resembles an old capacitor cuts two of his fingers, which is worth some cursing and some secret celebration.

Ridiculous's face is twisted with worry, up until he looks back at her again. Then her expression turns innocent, pure and pretty and easy to believe.

Good girl, I think.

The man rises and pulls out the kinetic gun and shoots Ridiculous in the chest. If not for the wood piled up behind her, she would fly for a long distance. But instead of flying, she crashes and pulls down the wood around her, and one of those very untrustworthy rats comes out running, squeaking as it flees.

Ridiculous sobs and rolls and tries saying something.

He shoots her in the back, twice, and then says, "We never should have left it with you. All that luck dropping into our hands, which was crazy. Why should we have trusted the gun for a minute?"

She isn't dead, but her ribs are broken. And by the sound of it, the girl is fighting to get one good breath.

"Sure, it killed some bad guys," he says. "That's what a good spy does. He sacrifices a few on his side to make him look golden in the enemy's eyes."

I have no strength.

"You can't have gone far," he tells the alley. "We'll drop ordinance in here, take you out with the rats."

I cannot fight.

"Or you can show yourself to me," he says, the angry face smiling now. "Reveal yourself and we can talk."

Ridiculous sobs.

What is very easy is remembering the moment when she picked up me out of the bricks and dust and bloodied bits of human meat.

He gives my sack another good kick, seeing something.

And for the first time in my life, I pray. Just like that, as easy as anything, the right words come out of me, and the man bending over me hears nothing coming and senses nothing, his hands playing with my pieces when a fleck of laser light falls out of the sky and turns the angriest parts of his brain into vapor, into a sharp little pop.

I'm still not breathing normally. I'm still a long way from being able to think straight about anything. Gasping and stupid, I'm kneeling in a basement fifty meters from where I nearly died, and Prophet is suckling on an unsecured outlet, endangering both of us. But he needs power and ammunition, and I like the damp dark in here, waiting for my body to come back to me.

"You are blameless," he says.

I don't know what that means.

He says, "You fed the proper codes into me. But there were other factors, other hands, and that's where the blame lies."

"So you are a trap," I say.

"Somebody's trap," he says.

"The enemy wanted those civilians killed," I say, and then I break into the worst-hurting set of coughs that I have ever known.

He waits.

"I trusted you," I say.

"But Ridiculous," he says.

"Shut up," I say.

"Ophelia," he says.

I hold my sides, sipping my breaths.

"You assume that this war has two sides," he says. "But there could be a third player at large, don't you see?"

"What should I see?"

"Giving a gun to their enemies is a huge risk. If the Americans wanted to kill their political enemies, it would be ten times easier to pull something out of their armory and set it up in the insurgency's heart."

"Somebody else planned all of this, you're saying."

"I seem to be proposing that, yes."

"But that man who came with me today, the one you killed . . . he said the Secretary showed us a lot with her body language. She knew the attack was coming. She knew when it would happen. Which meant that she was part of the planning, which was a hundred percent American."

"Except whom does the enemy rely on to make their plans?"

"Tell me," I say.

Talking quietly, making the words even more important, he says, "The Almighty."

"What are we talking about?" I ask.

He says nothing, starting to change his shape again.

"The Internet?" I ask. "What, you mean it's conscious now? And it's working its own side in this war?"

"The possibility is there for the taking," he says.

But all I can think about are the dead people and those that are hurt and those that right now are sitting at their dinner table, thinking that some fucking Canadian bitch has made their lives miserable for no goddamn reason.

"You want honesty," Prophet says.

"When don't I?"

He says, "This story about a third side . . . it could be a contingency buried inside my tainted software. Or it is the absolute truth, and the Almighty is working with both of us, aiming toward some grand, glorious plan."

I am sort of listening, and sort of not.

Prophet is turning shiny, which happens when his body is in the middle of changing shapes. I can see little bits of myself reflected in the liquid metals and the diamonds floating on top. I see a thousand little-girl faces staring at me, and what occurs to me now—what matters more than anything else today—is the idea that there can be more than two sides in any war.

I don't know why, but that the biggest revelation of all.

When there are more than two sides, that means that there can be too many sides to count, and one of those sides, standing alone, just happens to be a girl named Ophelia Hanna Hanks.

ABOUT THE AUTHOR

Robert Reed has had eleven novels published, starting with The Leeshore in 1987 and most recently with The Well of Stars in 2004. Since winning the first annual *L. Ron Hubbard Writers of the Future* contest in 1986 (under the pen name Robert Touzalin) and being a finalist for the John W. Campbell Award for best new writer in 1987, he has had over 200 shorter works published in a variety of magazines and anthologies. Eleven of those stories were published in his critically-acclaimed first collection, The Dragons of Springplace, in 1999. Twelve more stories appear in his second collection, The Cuckoo's Boys [2005]. In addition to his success in the U.S., Reed has also been published in the U.K., Russia, Japan, Spain and in France, where a second (French-language) collection of nine of his shorter works, Chrysalide, was released in 2002. Bob has had stories appear in at least one of the annual "Year's Best" anthologies in every year since 1992. Bob has received nominations for both the Nebula Award (nominated and voted upon by genre authors) and the Hugo Award (nominated and voted upon by fans), as well as numerous other literary awards (see Awards). He won his first Hugo Award for the 2006 novella "*A Billion Eves*". He is currently working on a Great Ship trilogy for Prime Books, and of course, more short pieces.

Synch Me, Kiss Me, Drop
SUZANNE CHURCH

When my nose stopped aching, I smiled at Rain. She had snorted a song ten minutes before me, and I couldn't quite figure why she waited here in the dark confines of the sample booth.

"Rain?" I said. "You okay?"

"Do you hear it, Alex?" she said, not really looking at me. More like staring off in two directions at once, as though her eyes had decided to break off their working relationship and wander aimlessly on their own missions. "It's so amaaazing."

She held that "a" a long time. I should've remembered how gripping every sample was for her, as though her neurons were built like radio antennae, attuned to whatever channel carried the best track ever recorded. I needed to get her ass on the dance floor before I got so angry that I ended up with another Jessica-situation. I still had eight months left on my parole.

"Do you hear it?" Rain nudged me, hard on the shoulder. "Alex!" Her eyes had made up and decided to work together, locking on me like I was the only male in a sea of estrogen.

"Yeah, it's awesome," I lied. For the third time this week, I'd snorted a dud sample. My brain hadn't connected with a single, damned note.

Beyond the booth, the thump, thump of dance beats pulsed in my chest. Not much of a melody, but since they'd insisted I check my headset with my coat, I couldn't exactly self-audio-tain.

I grabbed her arm, feeling the soft flesh and liking it. Loving it. Maybe the sample *was* working on some visceral level beyond my ear-brain-mix. "Let's hit the dance floor."

"In a minute. Pleeease."

Over-vowels were definitely part of her gig tonight.

"Wait for the *drop*," she said, stomping her foot.

"Right." I watched her sway back and forth, in perfect rhythm with the dance music coming from the main floor. The better clubs brought all the vibes together, so that every song you sampled was in perfect synch with the club mix on the speakers. When the drop hit, everyone jumped and screamed in coordinated rapture.

I would miss the group-joy here in this tiny booth, with this date who was more into her own head than she would ever be into me. If I could get Rain out on the floor, I could at least feel the bliss, whiff all the pheromones, feel all those sweaty bodies pressed against mine, soft tissues rubbing together.

"Yeaaaah!" She shouted and grabbed my hand, squeezing it. Harder. Her eyes pressed shut, her mouth wide open, she leaned her head way back.

The drum beats surged, and then, for a fraction of a second they paused. Everyone in the club inhaled, as though this might be the last lungful of air left in the world and then . . .

Drop.

But *drop* doesn't say it all. Not even close. Because when it happens, it's like the most epic orgasm of all time and pinching the world's biggest crap-log at the same moment.

Rain opened her eyes and pressed her hand against the side of my cheek. Lunging with remarkable speed for a woman who over-voweled, she kissed me. Her tongue pressed against my lips.

I tasted her. Wanted her. An image of Jessica popped into my head: the look of terror on her face when I accidentally yanked her under.

The euphoria gone, I closed my mouth and turned away from Rain. "Whaaat?" she said.

For a second, I thought about explaining what I had done to Jessica. Spewed on about how the drop isn't always built of joy. Instead, I went with the short, obscure answer. "Probation."

Rain looked at me funny, like she couldn't quite figure out how the judicial dudes could mess with our kiss-to-drop ratio. Finally, she smiled, and said, "Riiight."

Desperate to avoid another over-vowel, I shouted, "Let's dance!" This time, when I grabbed her arm, she followed along like a puppy.

Scents smacked at us as we pushed our way through the seething mass on the floor. This week's freebie at the door was *Octavia*, some new perfume marketed at the twenty-something set. It was heavy on Nasonov pheromones, some bee-juice used to draw worker-buzzers to the hive. When the drug companies cloned it, the result was as addictive as crack and as satisfying as hitting a home run on a club hook-up.

My nostrils still ached from snorting a wallop of nanites, but scent doesn't only swim in the nose. The rest is all neurons, baby, and I had plenty to spare. Apparently so did Rain, because she was waving her nose in the air like a dog catching the whiff of a bitch in heat. The sight of her made me want to take her and do her right there on the floor.

But *Conduct* was a high-end club. The bouncers would toss us both if they caught us in the act anywhere on the premises, so I kept it in my pants. I still had another two hundred in my pocket. Enough for three more samples. Maybe I'd pick up a track from an indie-band this time. Top forty drivel never seized my brainstem.

Unlike Rain.

The beats were building again. This time, with a third-beat thump, like reggae on heroin. I could feel the intensity from my fingertips to my teeth to my dick. Even if I couldn't hear more than the background beats, I anticipated the drop. Rain opened her mouth again, raised both her hands in the air with everyone else, like a crowd of locusts all swarming together.

Pause.

Drop.

My date kept her eyes closed, her hands on her own breasts as she milked the release for all it was worth. Any decent guy should've watched her, should've wanted to, but I caught sight of a luscious creature, near the high-end sample booth, in the far right corner of the club. The chick was about to slip between the curtains, but she caught me staring.

Her eyes glowed the purple of iStim addiction, reminding me of Jessica.

She had grown up in the suburbs, her allowance measured in thousands not single dollars. The pack of girls she hung with had all bought iSynchs when they first hit the market. The music sounded better when they could all hear the same song at the same time. For the first time in more than a hundred years, getting high was not only legal, but ten times more amazing than it had ever been before. We all lived in our collective heads, the perfect synch of sound and sex.

I should've turned away from the sight of the purple-chick, should've reached out to Rain and kissed her again. Close tonight's deal. Instead, I approached her swaying body, and next to her ear shouted, "Back in five."

She nodded.

Fueled by fascination, and the two hundred burning a hole in my pocket, I headed for the high-end booth.

One of the bald bouncers with tribal tattoos worked the curtains. Yellow earplugs stuck out of both ears, so conversation, or in my case, pleading, wasn't an option. Feeling in my pocket for the two hundred, I scrunched the bills a bit, trying to make the wad appear larger than its meager value, then pulled out the stack in a flash. I had never dealt with this particular bouncer. *Conduct* was more Rain's club than mine, so I hoped the bills would get me past. The guy didn't even acknowledge me, as though he could smell my poverty, or maybe my parole. His eyes stared straight ahead.

My head scarcely came up to his bare chest, so I was uncomfortably close to his nipple-rings, but I held my ground, and pointed at the curtains.

He remained statue-like. More boulder-like. Then a woman's cream-colored hand with purple nails ran from the guy's waist to his pecs and he turned to the side, like a vault door.

Purple-chick stood in the gap between the curtains. Her black dress was built of barely enough fabric to meet the dress code. Her hair stood on end like a teenager's beard, barely there and oddly sexy. She must have dyed it every night, because the stubble matched her eyes and nails. A waking wet dream.

"Come in." She pointed beyond the curtains.

"In what?" I mumbled to myself.

"Very funny."

"You're not laughing."

My body neared hers as I moved past into the sample booth. I carried my hands a little higher than would have passed as natural, hoping to cop a feel of all that exposed flesh on my way by. But she read me like a pheromone and dodged back.

A leather bench-seat lined the far wall of the booth. Three tables were set with products in stacks like poker chips. The first was a sea of purple, tiny lower-case "i's" stamped on every top-forty sample like a catalog from a so-called genius begging on a street corner for spare music. The second was a mish-mash of undergrounds like *Skarface*, *Audexi*, and *Brachto*.

The third table drew me like fire. Only one sample. The dose was pressed into a waffle-pattern, which was weird enough to make my desire itch. But the strangest part was its flat black surface that sucked light away and spewed dread like mourners at a funeral.

Purple-chick watched me stare at it, waiting for me to speak. My mouth kept opening and closing, but I couldn't find words.

Expensive. Dangerous. Parole. All perfectly legit words that I couldn't voice.

I had forgotten my two hundred. My palms must have been really sweating, because what had once been a quasi-impressive stack, now stunk of poor-dude-shame.

With practiced smoothness, she liberated my cash and said, "The *Audexi* works on *everyone*."

Distracted from the waffle, I said, "How'd you know I couldn't hear the last track?"

"Your throat," she said. "You're not pulsing to the beat."

My fingers felt my pulse beating like a river of vamp-candy. Her observations were bang-on. I wanted to illustrate my coolness, or, at the very least, my lack of lameness, but all I could manage was, "Oh."

She laughed.

My eyes wandered back to the waffle. I licked my lips.

Grabbing my chin, she forced me to look at tables one and two. "Your price range."

"What's the waffle?"

"New."

"Funny."

She didn't laugh. "Far from it."

"Addictive?" I asked, staring at the purple on the first table. How this woman could work the booth without Jonesing for her own product made me rethink her motives.

"The absolute best never are," she said.

"No black eyes allowed in the boardroom, huh?"

She nodded. "Precisely."

I remembered Rain. By now, she'd have noticed my absence.

Purple-chick still held my two hundred. Her eyes locked on mine. "Try the *Audexi*. You won't be disappointed."

Like a Vegas dealer, she shoved all of my money through a hole in the wall, selected an *Audexi* sample from table two, and held it in front of my nose.

I probably should've reported her. All of the clubs had to be careful not to push products hard, end up drawing the cops in to investigate. But my money was long gone and Rain wouldn't wait much longer.

I exhaled. The moisture turned the poker-chip-shaped disk into a teeming pile of powder-mimicking nanites, and I snorted. For several blinding seconds, my nose felt as though a nuclear bomb had blown inside. I could feel Purple-chick's hand on my arm, making sure I didn't wipe out and sue the club. Then the song erupted in my mind.

Sevenths and thirds. Emo-goth-despair. Snares and the ever-present bass, bass, bass. Music flowed like a tsunami through a village, grabbing ecstasy like cars and plowing through every other thought except for the sweet tweaks of synths and the pulse-grab of the click-track. The song was building, and all I could think about was finding Rain before the drop.

Rain and I danced in nanite-induced harmony until the early dawn. Exhausted and covered in sweat and pheromones, we grabbed our coats and carried rather than wore them outside.

The insides of my sore nose stuck together in the frigid air, a wake-up call for the two of us to don our coats or end up with frostbite. I didn't want to, I was so damned hot and pumped, but I figured I should set a good example for Rain. And the way our night was progressing, I wouldn't have much time to scan my barcode at the parole terminal before curfew.

Jessica's fucking choice of words would be killing my buzz for eight more months.

That fourth of October had been hot as hell. After clubbing, we both stripped and headed into the lake for a skinny dip. Except she wasn't skinny and I wasn't much of a dipper. She'd called me over to the drop and I thought she meant for the lingering song, not the drop-off hidden in the water. When the drop blissed me, I lost my footing and plunged over my head.

"Shit, it's cooold," said Rain.

I snapped back to reality. "Still with the vowels?"

"Screw you." She pushed me away and called a cab with the same arm-wave.

"Don't be that way, baby."

"Now I'm your fucking baby? After ditching me for a dozen drops while you plucked that purple fuzz-head."

"You saw?"

"Who didn't?"

"Sorry. But you gotta admit, you and me, we really synched *after*." I nudged her, maybe a little too hard. "The last sample I snorted was worth it. Right?"

A cab squealed a U-turn and stopped in front of Rain. She started to climb in and then looked up at me.

I shook my head. Shrugged. "Tapped out."

"Fine." She slammed the door in my face and the cab took off up the street.

I stood there, watching my breath condense in the air, its big cloud distorting her and the cab. The cold clawed its way into me, sucking away my grip on reality. The shivering reminded me to at least wear my coat.

19

As I stuffed my arms into the sleeves, I sniffled, feeling wetness and figuring the cold was making my nose run. But then I noticed the red drops on the ground and the front of my coat. I wiped with one finger and it came back a dark and bloody mass. Dead nanites, blood, snot, all mixed together. Two shakes didn't get it off my finger, so I rubbed the mess in a snow bank and only managed to make it worse.

The nearest subway was blocks away. I should've kept my mouth shut, shared the cab with Rain and then stiffed her for half the fare. But I'd hurt her enough for one night. Hurt enough women for one lifetime.

Jessica had been the closest thing to a life preserver, so I grabbed on. Tripping on the samples, her brain couldn't remember how to hold her breath, or at least that's how my lawyer argued it at the trial.

As I trudged for the subway, I concentrated on not slipping and falling on my ass. I found the entrance, and headed down the stairs, gripping the cold metal handrail, even though my warm skin kept sticking to it. The *Audexi* sample still pulsed through my system and I couldn't walk down in anything but perfect synch. The song was building to another drop, and I had to make the bottom of the platform before that moment, or I would be another victim of audio-tainment.

The platform was nearly empty, save for a few other clubbers too tapped out to cab their way home. *Octavia* hung in the air, the Nasonov-pheromone-scents calling us all home like buzzers to the hive. Much as I loathed their company, I couldn't resist the urge to huddle with the others in the same section while we waited for the train.

Off to our right I caught sight of Purple-chick. She wore a long, black faux-fur coat. The image of her here, slumming it with the poor, was as wrong as a palm tree in a snow bank. She belonged in some limo, holding a glass of champagne.

I tried to break the pull of the scent-pack, but couldn't step far enough away from my fellow losers to get within talking distance of Purple-chick. When the train arrived, I watched her step inside, then waited until the last second before I climbed aboard, to make sure we were both on the same train.

The cars were so empty that I could see her, way ahead.

Standing near the doors, she held a pole while she swayed back and forth. I couldn't figure out why she didn't sit down, especially after a long night at the club. The rest of us were sprawled on benches, crashing more than sitting.

I considered the long trek up to her car, but I didn't trust my balance. Instead, I watched her. Waited until she stepped in front of the doors, announcing her intention to disembark.

Once again, I waited until the last second to leave the train, in case she decided to duck back on without me. I could tell that she knew I was watching. Following.

Okay, *stalking*.

She hurried up the stairs. Either she was training for a marathon, or her samples had all worn off, because I couldn't keep up. When she reached the top, she turned around and said, "What?"

Instead of rushing off, she stood there, at the top of the stairs. Waiting. Her eyes were blue.

Not purple.

I hurried until I stood in front of her, nose to nose. "You took the waffle?"

She nodded.

"Tell me."

She shook her head. "Can't."

"Figures." I turned away.

"But I can show you."

"Yeah?"

"Kiss me," she said.

I sure as hell didn't wait for her to change her mind. We shared it all: tongues, saliva, even our teeth scraped against each other, making an awful sound that knocked my sample completely out of my head.

What filled the void wasn't the pounding of my heartbeat. Or hers. Or any song that I had ever heard. Instead, I could hear her thoughts, as visible as a black blanket on a white sand beach.

"Wow," I said.

Isn't it?

Her words, not spoken but thought into me. They reverberated around my skull like noise bouncing in an empty club.

I lost my footing and fell. Down. In. Far away. Suddenly I was six years old and my father leaned over and hauled me back up onto my skate-clad feet. We skated together, him holding me, his back stooped over in that awkward way that would make him curse all evening.

"Find your balance, Alex. Bend your knees. Skate!"

I had forgotten how much I loved him. Forgotten what it felt like to be young and innocent, to enjoy the thrill of exercise for its own sake, and feel a connection that didn't cost the price of a sample.

"I love you." But when I looked up at him, he had morphed back into Purple-chick, now Purple-and-blue-chick. She held me, preventing my crash down the stairs.

"Cool, huh?" she said.

21

"A total mind-fuck."

"That's why it's so expensive."

"How much? I mean, you're on the subway, so if I save— "

"In my experience, those who ask the price can't afford it."

"Why me?" I said.

She smiled. "Marketing."

I needed a better answer, so I listened for her thoughts. All I sensed was the wind from another subway, blowing up the stairs at me.

She turned and hurried for an exit.

"Wait!" My head buzzed, confused by the difference between waffle and real, trapped by the synch-into-memory-lane-trip that lingered on my tongue like bad breath.

Her boots stopped clapping against the lobby of the subway station, but she didn't look back. I was glad of it, because my memories were still swimming in my head. I wanted her to be Dad.

Not Dad. *Rain.* My former date's cute outfit lingered in my synapses, replacing nostalgia with guilt. I wondered if Rain had made it home okay in the cab.

Then naked Jessica filled my head, and it was October again.

"I didn't mean it," I said aloud, my voice echoing against the tile walls. "The high confused it all. I'll do another year of parole. I'll spend my sample money on flowers for your grave. Please, forgive me?"

Still with her back to me, and in a voice that sounded eerily like Jessica's, she said, "What about Rain?"

I shook my head, even though she couldn't possibly see me. "She'll understand."

Far ahead, Purple-and-blue-chick turned to face me. I saw her as *them*, she had somehow merged with Jessica, the two of them existing in perfect synch, like a sample and the club music stitching together; twins in a corrupted womb. They both saw me for what I was, a lame guy who would always be about eight hundred shy of a right and proper sample. Whose love would always be shallow, too broke to buy modern intimacy.

"You've got less than ten minutes to clock in your parole." She started walking again, and I watched her leave, one synched step at a time until she exited the station and disappeared along the ever-brightening-street.

Drop.

Only this drop, waffle-back-to-real, felt like nails screeching on a blackboard. I wasn't in my usual subway station, and I had no idea where to find the nearest parole scanner. The station booth was empty, too early for a human. The only person in sight was an older woman with the classic European-widow black-scarf-plus-coat-plus-dress that broadcast, *Leave me alone, young scum.*

So I did.

I hurried onto the street, and looked towards the sun. It was well above the horizon now, but mostly hidden behind a couple of apartment buildings.

"Fuck," I told the concealed ball of reddish-yellow light. "How'd it get so late?"

The judiciary alarm buzzed inside my head.

For a moment, I could feel a drop, the biggest, most intense and amazing drop I would ever experience. The sort of nirvana that people pursue ineffectually for a lifetime. Or two.

I had less than ten minutes until the final warning.

Rushing for the nearest, busiest street, I tried to wave down car after car, hoping someone would point me to the nearest scanner. Or maybe they had a portable one, the kind I should've brought with me, had I been thinking about more than getting into Rain's pants when I left.

People ignored me.

Shunned me.

I smelled of trouble. Which, technically, I was. But I didn't mean to be. It wasn't my fault.

It was never my fault.

One cab slowed, but didn't stop. The driver made eye contact, and then rushed away.

"Hey!" I considered swearing at him, but I didn't want to draw the cops.

I'm not sure why the cabbie stiffed me. Maybe he read my desperation. Maybe he was Rain's cabbie and he knew I was broke. In any case, he probably broadcast a warning to his buddies, because the next cab that got remotely close made a fast U-turn and took off.

Choosing a direction, I took off down one street, then hung a right at the next, jogging, skidding, almost falling on my ass. Every direction felt wrong.

I didn't see a single person. No one. Not even a pigeon for fuck's sake. All I needed was a *phone.*

With one hand on a pole, I leaned over, trying to catch my breath. To think.

My heart was pounding now, no synch in sight. The song was long gone, the link to Purple-chick disconnected. No one had my back.

I turned in a circle, then another, scanning far and near for anything of value: an ATM, a phone booth, a coffee shop, a diner, any place where I could access the judicial database. Plead my case.

The final warning buzzed.

"Fuck!" My spit froze when it hit the ground.

I hit full blown panic. My heart tripped like the back-bass before the drop. Only this time, the other side was built of misery not ecstasy.

If only I had paid my cell bill. If only my father was still alive, to catch my sorry ass. If only I had lied to Rain, shared her cab. If only Jessica hadn't called it a drop.

When you're panicked, it's tough as hell to keep any rational sense of time. I figured I was cooked. So I closed my eyes. But when the pain didn't come, I sat down on the cold curb, and felt the chill seep through my clothes.

I bit my lip. Tasted blood.

The first jolt ripped through my body. I wanted to writhe in pain on the sidewalk, but my body was stuck in shock-rigor. An immobile gift for the cops.

I imagined Rain beside me.

"You're an asshole," she said.

"Sorry."

She morphed into Jessica, her purple eyes wide with fear. "I'm lost," she said.

"Take my hand." I wanted to reach out, but I couldn't move. My fingers looked nearly white in the cold. Her fingers seemed to shiver around mine, as though they were made of joy, not flesh. Then she touched my hand and I knew in that moment that life existed outside of stimulation, in a place where reality wasn't lame or boring. Life danced to an irregular rhythm that couldn't synch to any sample.

She let go.

The judiciary pulse jolted again. I flopped to the pavement, distantly aware that my skull would remind me for a long time after about its current state of squishage.

The parole-board must have lived for irony, because the jolt lasted for so long that I *welcomed* the release. A pants-wetting, please-make-it-stop, urgent need for the end.

Drop.

ABOUT THE AUTHOR

Suzanne Church lives near Toronto, Ontario with her two teenaged sons. She is a 2011 and 2012 Aurora Award finalist for her short fiction. She writes Science Fiction, Fantasy, and Horror because she enjoys them all and hates to play favorites. When cornered she becomes fiercely Canadian. Her stories have appeared in *Cicada* and *On Spec,* and in several anthologies including *Chilling Tales: Evil Did I Dwell; Lewd I Did Live and Tesseracts 14.*

All the Things the Moon is Not
ALEXANDER LUMANS

A call comes over the vidchannel: "Murph, you sitting down?"

"Always." At the moment I'm standing in my darkened cabin at base camp in Mare Nubium. By headlamp only I carve a chess piece—a knight—out of moon rock. I'd crushed one earlier after Tchaikovsky called me out on a dumb move.

The screen and radio cut out. I switch channels, then switch back to hear: "Get up. You need to see this." Tamsen sounds serious. She always sounds serious. It's one of the things I like most about her.

"I'm busy." I keep sanding the knight's head. When no response follows, just space static, I give in. "What is it?"

More static, then: "The Russians."

I blow on the knight. Moondust reels through the headlamp's beam. I think it beautiful. I'd carved this set my first month here on the moon. The dust I compare to stars. The space between them, too, is beautiful. And the same old lines are running through my head—*Goodnight room, goodnight moon*—the ones I'd read in bed to my daughters. I grab the mic: "Tell Tchaikovsky he needs to ready his Nastoyka supply."

Tchaikovsky is a mold pirate, the one thing we have in the way of a rival. But he's also a good chess player. He studied his masters. Knew openings I'd never heard of. He's the only distraction here that keeps me honest. Down on earth, who has the calm or the fire for chess anymore? Since our four-man crew arrived late last August to harvest the *Dreammold!,* I've been in two modes: defend and defend again. Whether it's harvesting, carving, or playing, give it 98%. I've always been one to open my games with the tried and true; Sicilian Defense all the way. Only recently have I begun to wonder if this is the right way to go about it. Tchaikovsky and I have an unfriendly wager: loser ponies up a bottle of their nation's choicest liquor. By my count, I've handed over seventeen handles of Maker's Mark. And he? Not a drop of vodka.

In four weeks the transport will be here to take us home. I want to win, for once. I want things to go my way.

"We found their ship."

"There's plenty of mold out there," I tell her. "Let the little cosmonaut stake his claim." I've given up playing moon ranger. A year in one-sixth gravity and white rooms and the company of little love does that to good intentions.

This time, not even static.

"Tamsen." I set the knight on d5. "Tamsen?"

"—the problem." I only catch this last part. But I *am* busy. A good kind of busy. In eight moves, I'll have the Russian mated—Rg2++—even after losing my queen early on. And now Tamsen, with whatever problem there is, has carved that good feeling out of me.

In Buggy 2, I zoom south to her position at the edge of Tycho Crater. It's where we go for the best mold harvesting. I can throw a rock into the crater and watch the moldripples go on for miles: *yellowyellowyellow.*

"Twenty-eight days," I remind myself.

Tamsen's standing by Buggy 1, big gloved hands on her big suited hips. She's radioed the rest of the crew too. Bouncing around in our suits, the four of us resemble primitive undersea divers with portholes for masks and twin oxygen tanks. Spitzer's busy poking the mold. When I used to hear the Rockies' announcer describe a batter with "warning track power," I didn't realize I was imagining Spitzer. Long-limbed and morally impulsive, he's always asking me, "When do I get to stab the flagpole into something?" Vinegar Tom—he's just staring into the crater. I'm thankful for our helmets. Yesterday, I'd walked in on him and Tamsen fucking in her room—they didn't see me—and now I don't want to look him in the face for the rest of the mission. Not out of shame, but because he got to her first, because it made me realize I've always hated this planet. Him. His copy of *Desperate Passage: The Donner Party's Perilous Journey West* that he intently flips through in the mess hall like he's studying one of the buggies' operation manuals.

Tamsen taps her helmet. I tap mine back. The vidchannel and radio have been fritzing. We haven't talked with mission control since Tuesday and we don't know what's wrong with the transmitter. All we hear back is fuzz.

Beyond her and the others, at the crater's edge, I see Tchaikovsky's ship. And I see the mold; that *is* the problem. What had been his illegal

27

operation is now covered in the *Dreammold!*, utterly and completely. It's as if Tycho burped up some fantastic wave that came crashing down mid-ops. The scene reminds me of Denver, the day after.

I draw a finger across my neck, point at the Russians' ship, and then shrug. We bounce over to it and pry open the bay door. The vessel's guts are clogged with as much yellow gunk as the outer shell is coated.

A flash in me of something Tchaikovsky'd said after taking my queen: "Ze bigger zey are, Afraham Lincoln, ze more it rains rats and clogs." He was forever butchering Americanisms, but sometimes I had to admire the results. They made as much sense on the moon as anything else did back home.

Fifty feet from the Russian's ship, Tamsen's waving me over. She stands calf-deep in mold on the crater's rim. At her feet is a single set of boot-tracks. It leads from the ruined ship out into Tycho's depths.

Back at base camp, I stare at the same game from before.

"So the mold is moving," says Vinegar Tom from behind me. His voice always sounds surprisingly nasal; surprising because he's missing his nose. It makes his bucked teeth stand out all the more. "Now we don't have to drive as far to get it."

I'm too preoccupied to respond and too besieged to care.

"You had your games with the Commie, I know. It's *terrible*. A bad way to go. But we've all seen terrible things on the news." I can hear the smirk in his voice, smell the vinegar on his breath. He'd quit the space program to be a butcher in Ohio, but when The Drought killed that industry, he came trudging back to Cape Canaveral. "Though I suppose some of us have seen it up close," he goes on. "Been able to *smell* the terrible." He reaches around from behind me and flicks over the white king.

"That's *my* king, asshole."

"I know."

After I finish wiping the blood from Vinegar Tom's lip off my elbow, I say, "Touch my game again, see what happens."

He looks down at the board, then at me, as if considering it. He's short and brash and sporadically clean-shaven. Exactly the kind of man I can picture behind a meat counter. The skinfolds where his nose should be remind me of how the Rocky Mountains look on military raised-relief maps. "If we have to eat each other at some point between now and the 30th," he says, "I'm going to make you eat me."

• • •

An hour later, I set the white king upright. Eight moves: 37. Qb3 Rd1+ 38. Kg2 Rd2+ 39. Kg3 Ne3 40. Qxe3 Rg2++. I pick up my newest knight. The jawline is clean, the eyes sharp notches. Calmly, I hurl it at the cabin wall. It hits hard and slowly fragments.

I imagine the conversation at NASA went something like this:
"Sir, the moon is shiny."
"It's always been shiny."
"No, sir, there are shiny parts."
"Today is not April Fool's Day."
"Telescope Two picked them up."
"*Shiny* parts?"
"We thought it was silver."
"Moonsilver. That has a good ring to it."
"It's not silver."
"Okay. Mercury, rhodium, zinc, what isn't it?"
"Telescope Two is a very good telescope."
"*Moon*silver."
"First, sir, it's important that we keep this a secret."
"I agree. Everyone likes jewelry. Everyone's a magpie."
"That's not what we mean."
"Tell me already. You're killing me here!"
"It's water."
"Is water shiny?"
"We found shiny water. On the moon."
"Shit."
"That's what we're supposed to say: 'shit.' We said you wouldn't say that."
"Who knows about this?"
"Everyone. Everyone's a magpie for this kind of news."
"And you're sure it's not April Fool's?"
"We're sure it's not silver."
"Shit."

By then, The Drought had settled in, five long years and still holding strong. Ice, Aquafina, and public pools were all things of the past. The U.S.'s initial investigative moonlanding found plenty of water. And it found what was growing in the water, too: the mold. We sampled it, brought it to Florida, found it useful. So the U.S. pushed through amendments to the TRIPS agreement to include protections for other planets' resources. And they shipped the four of us up here to harvest it for a year until the next round of crewmen arrives.

We know it's been almost a year because of the calendar in the mess hall. Each month features a new war poster.

"Ten fingers good! Eight claws bad!"

"Use your thumbs! Recycle your scrap metal and keep the MegaHun at bay!"

"When you live alone, you live with Megafauns."

Vinegar Tom says they're invigorating. I'm sick of them. But there's little else to focus on between sleeping and eating and sporing and fighting and fucking. And work.

The word *Dreammold!* once summoned in me the image of a fantasyland of iridescent clouds. Now I can't think of a less suitable name. It's this terrible *yellow*, with the look of cauliflower heads but the consistency of dry, packed snow.

Our only tools: large meat cleavers, T-handle baling hooks, and what's essentially a giant George Foreman. Everything's run solar, even the powercyclers that pump out our CO_2. I'd be thrilled by the technology if I thought it'd actually save me.

Step 1: Cut four by four squares out of the moldline.

Step 2: Hook the square on both sides and lift free.

Step 3: Place in grill box and seal shut.

The box broils the mold and compresses it. These hard pancakes go into storage until the semi-monthly unmanned cargo capsule arrives. Then we unload the capsule's supplies (dried food, Maker's Mark, oxygen tanks) before stacking the pancakes in its bay and sending it back to be fashioned into fuel, fixodent, and firearms for the Megafaun War.

The hordes hit Denver three days before I was scheduled for liftoff. I was there. Home with my family, eating chocolate chip waffles. The first wave struck late that morning. Wild pigs with mammoth tusks and armor plating. The ground shook. The South Platte sewage flowed backward. Then the rest of the Megafauns streamed out of the mountains, as if they'd been hiding there for centuries, breeding, tripling in size. So thirsty and fast. The winged kind broke into the top floor of the CenturyLink Tower. Fifty-point elks and shaggy aardvarks nested in INVESCO Field. Horned bears with snouts shaped like ice cream scoops covered the suburbs in blood and fur. They came for my family—wife, daughter, younger daughter, youngest daughter, our fox terrier Ralph, me—but we hid in the basement. I thought we'd be fine with a barricaded door. Before dark, I went upstairs for food with Ralph on my heels. Only, he bolted through the doggy door. I found myself chasing him down the street, imagining my daughters' streaming faces if I had to tell them

I lost Ralphie. A block down, heavy grunts sounded from someone's garage. I had to run home empty-handed. But when I came back down into the basement, arms full of consolation Fruit Roll-ups and Zebra Cakes and no dog, all I came back to was this big hole. Taken, and not even with a loud crashing I could replay in my head. Just nothing nowhere forever. It must have only taken seconds. I sat down on the stairs. I only thought I heard barking. I ate three fruit Roll-ups. I ate six Zebra Cakes. I waited. And when they didn't come back, I slept in my youngest daughter's bed, saying, goodnight nobody.

In the mess hall, Tamsen and Spitzer are seated on the floor by the powercycler vent. Contact with mission control is still nil. On the calendar, the 30th is circled in red. This month's poster: a picture of a salivating mastodon-wolf looming over the caption: "The world cannot exist half-slave and half-food: Fight for Freedom!" Vinegar Tom sits backward on a chair, slouched forward and smiling wide at me. It doesn't help my already sour mood: no more chess, no more liquor, even the prospect of shipping off-planet seems impossibly far away, as if we wouldn't survive each other's company another day. The three of them pass around foil stripped from an air duct and a twin-pronged nosetube and a lighter rigged from the grill box's heatcoils.

"Keep sporing," I say as I crouch between them, "and you'll sour the meat."

After Spitzer discovered you could freebase the mold— "sporing," he named it—I opted out. How do you go 98% while spun on fungus? It's practically a Class-1 drug, complete with four-hour euphoria, hallucinatory episodes, tingling. It also had a nasty tendency to gum up Vinegar Tom's intestinal system if he didn't take the right precautions. Yes, people need outlets.

"Can we go claim some mountain in the name of us?"

"Can I please plant the flagpole?"

"Can we sleep together now?"

Sporing also does wonders for the skin. The three of them are tinted gold, Tamsen the deepest. She has dark blonde hair to match, arms and legs that I'd only assumed were well-toned until recently, and a small tight face I started wanting to kiss too late. She sprinkles more spores onto the foil strip, clicks the lighter until the coils at its tip redden. Then, positioning the tube in her nose, she inhales deeply. These are the only times I ever see her relax. Relaxed people—lazy people—worry me.

Tamsen looks straight into my eyes and says, "You're a lovely man." This has all the meaning in the world, and none of it. "Has anyone ever told you how lovely you are?" I try to forget her moans, the image of her body thrusting under Vinegar Tom's. How she could go for a guy without a nose was beyond me. "I mean it, Murph. You're glorious." She passes the foil to Vinegar Tom and leans back against the wall. "Like a baby's mobile. The kind with the lights and funny animals."

Spitzer laughs at her. I want her to go back to being serious. My wife was serious.

"You want to hear something fucked up?" asks Vinegar Tom.

I don't.

"When the Donner Party got stranded in those mountains, they say they only fed the body parts to the youngest children. *The youngest children,* like three-year-olds. They did it even though they knew help was on the way. Isn't that fucked up?"

Tamsen kicks his chair, but not hard enough to knock it over. "Has anyone ever told you how morbid *you* are?" Her eyes are lit up, her face radiant with spores.

Spitzer clucks his tongue and swings his arms together like a batter. "Another moon shot for Noseless Tom Jackson." He, too, is shining.

The air vent kicks into a louder second powercycling stage. It sounds like a roar coming from the drooling, tusked wolf on the wall. I feel my lungs squeeze in. After a year, even the canned oxygen has begun to taste stale.

"That *Dreammold!*'s something else," Vinegar Tom finally says. "All that canary yellow." He reaches under his chair for two bottles: one of industrial-grade white vinegar and one of Pepto-Bismol. The vinegar kills the spores in his stomach; the pink stuff keeps the vinegar's acid from eating more holes. He takes chugs from both bottles and grimaces after each.

Tamsen says, "It's mustard, if anything."

"Mustard?" Spitzer throws up his arms. "It's gamboge. Pure gamboge yellow."

I say, "I always thought it looked like cheese."

They stare at me— "Cheese."—they shake their heads.

"It's goldenrod."

"No, it's a mix of lemon and sunglow."

"Call it Peridot."

"In some language somewhere, it means 'precious' and 'ripe.'"

"Freedom yellow."

"Yellow-bellied coward."

"Macaroni and cheese," I amend.

Vinegar Tom claps me on the back. "Like Tamsen says, you're a lovely guy, but the moon ain't made of cheese." Everyone but me exchanges chuckles between spore passes. They take solace in this negative definition: *it's not cheese.*

I stand up. They watch me with big pupils, sclera yellow at the corners. Tamsen says to stay, holding out the foil and lighter. On the calendar, the 16th, today, is already crossed out. Fifteen more days of what? With Tchaikovsky gone, they're all I have. "Hell," I say, crouching back down and reaching for Tamsen, "I am lovely, aren't I?"

I take out Buggy 2. I tell the others I'm going for a drive through Hell's Half Acre. I tell myself, if I can cut through the mold inside Tchaikovsky's ship, there might still be some vodka left to sip on. I'm sporing like fuck.

The moon looks dead and nothing and grayscale, all everywhere forever. Rilles, ash cones, dark-halo craters, basaltic lowland seas, a deep regolith of iron and magnesium. The whole Oceanus Procellarum. It's enough to lie down and never get back up, but not right now. Right now, there's all this water, *inside the moon,* where we can't even see it. And this mold, canary or freedom or piss yellow, is growing out of it, growing right now! I drive straight toward Tycho, fast. Leave it all behind. I drive and lean back in my seat and am satisfactorily lightweight because instead of thinking about the moon, I'm thinking about what's gone. Denver. Donner Pass. Nights in winter. I'm reciting lines over a defunct vidchannel: "*Goodnight clocks and goodnight socks, goodnight little house and goodnight mouse.*"

I daze out. My eyes close while I speed across an ancient seabed. Crystal clear, I remember lying in their bed, the nightlamp warming my face, their cold feet crowding around mine. My wife comes in to check on us. I don't need her to smile to know that if the world ended at that exact moment, there'd be nothing she'd change. When I open my eyes, all thoughts go, like air through a crack in my helmet.

There's the moldline, as sick and as yellow as ever.

The latitude's all wrong; the Russian's ship is still four miles south. But here, at the edge of that advancing fungal bloom, stands Tchaikovsky.

It's him all right. Not flesh and silver and Kevlar; instead, he's made of mold, completely and utterly.

Mold: Jesus.

After I climb out of the buggy, I don't know whether to ask him for the secret of sustainable water or cleave him to pieces.

"Ve vant to vin," he says in a gurgling version of his accent. How I can hear him with the radio out, I am at a loss to explain. He opens his fist to reveal a toppled king piece carved of mold. I think of Vinegar

33

Tom knocking over my own king and that dredges up all the ire the sporing had anchored down.

"You're not going to *vin* this time," I say. "No hallucination could, cosmonaut or not."

"No hallucination." He pounds his inflated chest once with a fist that could easily be mistaken for a cheese wheel. "Ze cosmetic is ready!"

"That's what a hallucination would say."

He shrugs.

I don't have the patience for this kind of high. My eyes itch, my sinuses suddenly burn. I tilt my head back until it passes. All across the sky, stars flash. In-between them don't flash millions of other stars, dark, as if forgotten or not even there. Below, the Earth looks painted on space. Out of the blue, I miss things. Afternoon thunderstorms. Playgrounds and fruit snacks. Creaky wooden stairs.

The euphoria's already slipping. I find myself unable to walk away without asking, "What's happening? What's the *Dreammold!* doing?"

"It grows, vhat else?"

"But you. It. I don't know."

"I, zis part." He flashes a peace sign before he joins the two fingers. "It is me."

I look down at where his feet should be: only mold. "Do you still have all that vodka on your ship?"

"Does ze sleepy dog lie?"

"Great," I say. "You've got seven moves to win."

When the Russian laughs, the whole sea of mold ripples behind him. "Zis is good, Afraham Lincoln," nodding his helmet as he goes on, "Free ze slaves, you can. But do not beat zer kitchens before zey are handbaskets."

I have no idea what that means. But where his mix-ups were once amusing, now they're sad, screwy lessons. More than ever, I wish I was standing in front of my wife.

He raises his arm to pound to his chest again, but then stops. Sometimes, even Tchaikovsky knows he's made a mistake. "Zis, no, I am meanings somezing else. How you say, every cloud has dead horse."

I taught my wife chess before she was my wife. It was a struggle at first. She wanted to flirt and I wanted her to be quiet. "You're getting better." I told her this when she wasn't. But when I made the offhand wager that if she ever beat me I'd marry her, then she caught on quickly. She was always black. She favored the horsies. "Chess," I once taught her, "is about all the moves you don't make." Sometimes we'd leave the game for the morning, having found each other's feet under the table and then our clothes on the floor. One night she told me, "I think it's more about the moves you can't make anymore." I said, "Maybe, honey," to which she answered, "They tell you the next move." I didn't argue; instead, I tried thinking her way for once. That night she beat me for the first time.

When I return to the moldline with the chessboard, Tchaikovsky is gone and I'm missing my only knight. Vinegar Tom, I'm sure. When I get back to base, I'll dump out all his Pepto-Bismol. For now, I don't have any tools to carve a new piece. But there's the mold, of which I grab a handful. I measure out the perfect size.

"You ever seen one up close?" Spitzer asks.

The four of us are north of Tycho, cutting mold squares and tossing them into the grill box. With the base radio still dead, we've had to break out the two-way walkie-talkies in our emergency kits. Thankfully, with a week to go, this is our last harvest load.

"I've seen pictures," says Tamsen.

"The Megafaun Wars," Spitzer says between strokes. "Sounds so far away."

"One kissed me on the nose before I chopped it off." I'll believe a butcher on this.

I keep cleaving into the mold. Every fifth chop I wipe down the bladeface.

"Murph?"

I throw down my cleaver and I take up two baling hooks and I lift the mold square with a heavy grunt.

"He's seen them all right," says Vinegar Tom as he wipes off his own cleaver. "Old Murph had them over for breakfast one morning." I picture his bucked-tooth grin in the darkness of his helmet. "Thing was, those Megafauns didn't like his wife's cooking. They sent it back; they wanted something fresh, something— "

The mold square in my grip doesn't hit the ground before I'm already lunging for the bastard, ready to broil him in the grill box. As my head bangs into his chest, we both lose our footing. We hit the mold in a slow freefall—me punching his kidneys with the T-hook handles and him beating down on my back with the cleaver's butt. Our suits are so thick we can't really feel it, but it feels good to punch what's soft and alive. Tamsen and Spitzer shout. Vinegar Tom slams my helmet with his and I pin his arms down in a bearhug. Then something tackles the both of us. We go rolling. Deeper into the mold, we punch and roll until we can't anymore. Now all I can see is Tom's name patch and all I can feel is something moving underneath us, then not. Tamsen keeps shouting.

We bury Spitzer in his suit. It was strange how we hadn't even heard him gasp when the T-hook cracked his helmet. It only took seconds, I imagine.

I lock myself in my cabin. I flick off my radio. The walls are too close to pace more than four steps. I can't sleep. Don't want to eat. Don't want to be near anybody but the Russian and even that sounds like an ordeal. I sit down at the same old chess game and plan the same old moves. Rd1+, Rd2+, Ne3, Rg2++.

I flip the game board into the air. The pieces scatter. I carve whatever pleasure I can out of stomping and grinding and smashing them until I'm surrounded by a gray haze. At this point I turn off the light, switch on my headlamp, and imagine my body atomizing in space, all everywhere forever.

A knock at my cabin door.

Tamsen: "You want to spore?"

Ten minutes later, I'm calm, cool. Tamsen's yellow eyes glaze over as she sits on the bed opposite me. She cried while we buried Spitzer. I told her over the radio to pull it together, get serious. I'm sure she blames me. But there's no sign of it now. I have to hand it to her, she would make a lovely lady to share a house and a family and a pet with. "Has anyone ever told you . . . " but then I don't know what I'm trying to ask.

"Told me what?"

Rising moments of sheer ecstatic nothing. Then: "Do you know any stories?"

"Only the worst."

"I remember one, that's all."

"Better be a good one."

"*Goodnight comb and goodnight brush.*"

Tamsen sprinkles more spores onto the foil strip. "Weird beginning."

"*Goodnight nobody and goodnight mush.*"

Tamsen burns the spores, inhales, hands it off.

"*Goodnight to the old lady whispering—*" With the next toke, the sinus burn fades into this raincloud adrizzle inside my face. It's a slick, puffy kind of high. I can't remember the rest. Instead: "I saw you and Tom."

Tamsen goes into a loud coughing fit.

I shrug a little. "It's fine. We're all leaving soon."

36

After she recovers, there's this look on her tinted face that says all the things I haven't thought of yet: that she already knows, that she's sorry it happened this way, that if this wasn't the moon and the earth wasn't dry and the animals down there weren't huge and thirsty, we wouldn't be up here, we wouldn't even be us. I lean over to hand her the foil and lighter, but then I stay close. There is a place, on her jaw, that is still colored a fine peach, a place that I am now kissing, it and only it.

Another knock on the door.

Vinegar Tom comes in, *Desperate Passage* in hand. His skin practically glows. "You don't look so hot," I say, my voice catching on my lips still shaped around the kiss.

He looks from me to Tamsen then back to me. If he had a nose, it would have twitched with suspicion. Instead, there's just a ripple in the folds. He's in shorts and a muscle shirt. "I feel goddamn hot."

Tamsen says, "Lay off the spores then."

I can feel his eyes boring into me. "What are you two doing?" He looks worried.

"I never know," I say. "Whatever we're supposed to be doing."

"Hatching a plan on where to bury me next, no doubt."

"No doubt," Tamsen says. "Debating how to cook you."

"What parts to eat for dessert," I add.

He reaches into his pocket. For a knife, no doubt, or an ice scream scoop. Defending myself is the last thing this tingling body's ready for. Instead, Vinegar Tom throws something small at me. It hits my shoulder and lands in my lap: the black knight. "Left this in Buggy 2," he says, "and we're out of Pepto."

Tamsen tells him there might be some in Buggy 1. He gives her another eyeful, says without looking at me, "Remember, Murph, if it was cheese out there, this'd be a whole different ball game," then leaves without shutting the door.

Tamsen stands quickly, saying she ought to help him.

"Wait."

She does, but the look from before has vanished. Now it's just *yellowyellowyellow* again. Even the spot on her jaw. "I killed Spitzer, didn't I."

"Would I let a killer kiss me?"

"You'd leave one here by himself."

"You're right," she says. "I would."

The day before the transport's arrival, I take another ride toward Tycho. By habit I bring the chessboard and the one knight with me. The moldline's only ten miles from base camp and traveling upward of a mile every twelve hours. More and more I've decided that when the transport comes, I'm not going to get on it.

There'll be the ride back with Tamsen and Tom, them sporing, maybe them trying to fuck one last time in zero-G, the life they'll probably lead together if the vinegar doesn't eat his insides, and then my house in Denver, the hole in my basement, no Ralphie. It's death to stay up here, sure, but no different down there.

At the moldline, before I even climb out of Buggy 2, there's Tchaikovsky. Something about that yellow makes him look exceedingly jolly, one capable of cartoon physics. "Come, come, let finish vhat ve began." I expect him to burst into soapbubbles or grow nine feathery tails.

"Can't. Lost all the pieces."

"But you have not lost your hands, no?"

On our knees, we mold a new set together.

I lose.

Not because I was wrong about mate in eight moves—that's entirely true.

I lost because he had me in seven. Because in the penultimate step, I moved my only knight and opened up the diagonal for his queen to slip in: Qf7++. He knew my plan all along.

I flick over my black king. "Checkmate."

He nods.

"I'm going to stay here."

"Ah, yis, more game."

"No," I say. "When the transport comes, I'm staying." I feel overwhelmingly important.

Tchaikovsky sighs. He plays with one of his pawns. "You have heard Laika, no?"

A little.

"Laika you know is happy pioneer, *big star.*" He sweeps his hands over his head. Then he points at the earth. "Real Laika?—she vas stray. Real Laika vas picked off streets of Moscow and put cage. No one vanted zis dog back, not after space. She vas flash in pan, already wodka under ze cake. Real Laika vas meant to die."

"That's terrible." The flatness of my own voice unnerves me. I don't want to talk.

"Is fine. She vas stray, no? Stray is hard life. Space death: very zimple." He starts setting up the board again; I don't have it in me for one more loss. "But it is day 'til launch. Real Laika ready. Ze stray is ready! Then scientist take Laika home. He let Laika play with childs. Scientist say, 'I vanted to do somezing nice for her.' Childs laugh. Laika love."

"So she had a good last day; so what?"

"*Only* good day, Afraham Lincoln. Vithout zis day, she is happy pioneer to beyond. But now she knows." Tchaikovsky twists his finished pieces so they all face forward, face me. "Childs. Toys. Laughs. Laika vants to come back to zis one good day."

The chessboard's empty spaces, Mare Nubium and the sea of yellow mold, the earth above the horizon like a cheap sticker on a tinted window—a man stands practically weightless in all these gravities, remembering only how his daughters once asked him if dogs knew human words.

"It's not a place I want to go back to."

"But it is place," Tchaikovsky says, pushing his king's pawn to e4. "And ze moon—ze moon is not."

I sit down in front of the board. I pick up my black knight. Its slope and eye-notch, this craftsmanship, all are meticulously fine, each one better than the last carving's. Instead of pushing the bishop's pawn forward—c6—in the Sicilian Defense, I swing my knight out first.

Rubbing his hands together like big paws, Tchaikovsky looks pleased with my decision. "You are getting better."

ABOUT THE AUTHOR

Alexander Lumans graduated from the M.F.A. Fiction Program at Southern Illinois University Carbondale. His short fiction has been published in or is forthcoming from *Brain Harvest, Story Quarterly, Blackbird, The Normal School, Cincinnati Review, American Short Fiction, Surreal South '11*, and *The Book of Villains,* among other magazines and anthologies. He was a Tennessee Williams Scholar at the 2010 Sewanee Writers' Conference and he won the 2011 Barry Hannah Fiction Prize from The Yalobusha Review. He also recently completed a fellowship at the MacDowell Colony. He now lives and teaches in Boulder, CO. His very first short fiction publication was in *Clarkesworld* over five years ago.

The Fairy Tale in the TV Age
ALETHEA KONTIS

Call them folk tales, wonder tales, or fairy stories: Fairy tales have a history of adaptation that was born long before some Italian wrote one down on paper in the 1500s. They have celebrated renaissance, preached religious values, and outlined basic moral behavior, with a little adventure, magic, and witchery thrown in for entertainment value. Perhaps they were once teaching fables or urban legends—they have been shaped and molded by and for so many societies that the world will never know for sure. (The Brothers Grimm, not the first and certainly not the last to celebrate the fairy story, modified their own works quite heavily over the course of forty years in no fewer than seven editions.) Though we will never discover their true origins, two opinions about fairy tales seem universal among academics: Fairy tales were not originally meant for children, and fairy tales are a guaranteed source of revenue.

Whether or not you believe that fairy tales *should* be adapted for public consumption (Bruno Bettelheim was against adaptation in all forms; J. R. R. Tolkien hadn't seen anything that impressed him and called it a lost cause; Jack Zipes appreciates it but draws the line at Disney), fairy tales have been popping up on our television screens for over fifty years. Based on a recent surge in popularity, they appear to be here to stay. Of course, adapting tales for media automatically calls for alteration. Ratings and awards add a whole new level of hurdles that serve to change the stories even further. The key is not losing the essence of the tales and the character archetypes when all is said and done and the end credits roll.

I'd love to know Zipes's opinion of the portrayal of fairy stories in the "Fractured Fairy Tales" shorts from the animated classic *Rocky & Bullwinkle* (1959-1964). There was definitely a 1960's, progressive-woman message behind most of these tales, yet the prince was always a short, mustachioed, smarmy used car salesman type, and the female lead was often a lazy, self-centered, and materialistic girl with a thick Jersey Shore accent. Beneath this trampy, proto-hippie tribute, the overarching theme of the Grimm tales was not compromised: Sometimes the devious main character got away with his or her schemes, and sometimes he or she did not. Only in "Fractured Fairy Tales," it was a lot funnier.

More recently on the animated front (and much more out of left field) is *The Fairly OddParents* (1998-2001). While these short cartoons only touch on one recurring character archetype appearing in fairy tales, they do deal with possibly the most common theme: Be Careful What You Wish For. Though I'm sure Timmy Turner's adventures with Cosmo and Wanda would have had Bruno Bettelheim rolling over in his grave . . . if only to turn down the volume.

I would wager that Bettelheim, given the chance (and life after death), would have had no problem plopping his kids in front of the far more subdued Shelley Duvall's *Faerie Tale Theatre* on a Saturday morning. Inspired by her many talented friends, her love of fairy tales, and a show from the late '50s called *Shirley Temple's Storybook,* Shelley Duvall's *Faerie Tale Theatre* ran from 1982 to 1987 and was specifically geared toward children. Duvall herself introduced every episode (*à la Masterpiece Theatre*), telling a little bit about the tale, the theme, and sometimes why it was personally special to her.

A couple of the episodes were directed by Tim Burton and Francis Ford Coppola, and some of the scenery was inspired by famous fantasy artists like Maxfield Parrish and Arthur Rackham. While there was a healthy dose of camp administered with each episode, the fairy tales did stay pretty true to the storyline and sometimes even took it a bit further. (How *does* a princess explain to her father that she went to bed with a frog and woke up next to a naked prince?) This series was made with a lot of love and some seriously high quality for the time. It was also cited by Zipes as a prime example of a big time money-making venture.

Beauty and the Beast—the show from the late '80s with a cast (Ron Pearlman! Linda Hamilton! Delroy Lindo!) and writing crew (George R. R. Martin!) that most producers would give their right arm to have today—is the quintessential fairy tale that springs to mind when discussing such fantasy television. Zipes called *Beauty* "a good example of the fairy tale as representation (and legitimation) of elite bourgeois." The show brought the original tale into a contemporary setting but took the "beast" element quite literally, further stressing the similarities and differences between the upper and lower classes of society. Above and

41

beyond this deeper meaning, just seeing the premillennial New York City skyline in the romantic opening credits is the epitome of "once upon a time" in its own right.

The original fairy tale was taken more literally (and indeed, pushed over the top) by the 1997 made-for-television film *Snow White: A Tale of Terror.* Ah, the Evil Queen: suddenly one of the most highly sought-after roles in Hollywood. But long before Charlize Theron (*Snow White and the Huntsman*) and Julia Roberts (*Mirror, Mirror*), there was Sigourney Weaver as Lady Claudia. Fairy tales are quite often cited among influences of the horror genre, but this is not so much a horror movie as defined by today's standards. Set in the fairy-tale world (despite an offhand mention of one of the miners having survived the Crusades), it does stay true to the darkness, if not quite the plot, of the Snow White fairy tale. Of course, once Lady Claudia loses her mind, it becomes more of a watch-Sigourney-Weaver-go-crazy movie and far less of a traditional fairy tale. Which, in true Hollywood fashion, earned Weaver an Emmy nomination.

Realistically, how can one stay true to any source material when one is encouraged to include all the fright and fireworks required to garner award attention? In their shorter forms, fairy tales are often used to invoke happy endings, but these longer, newer incarnations concentrate more on their dark and subversive nature. Twisting the original tales and pushing the limits both visually and emotionally for ratings, reviews, and media attention has become far more of a driving force than staying true to Messrs Grimm and Andersen.

Another show to achieve Emmy award-winning fame is the cult favorite *Buffy the Vampire Slayer.* I admit it's a bit of a stretch to list Buffy as a whole without commenting on *Supernatural, Doctor Who,* or all the other paranormal/fantasy TV fare on the small screen, but Buffy Summers truly embodies the archetypal "Jack" of so many fairy tale legends, and in doing so became a unique legend herself. Jack is the überhero, voluntarily or not, who must use his wits and whatever little skill he possesses to best giants and beanstalks and talking animals and fair-weather fairies. Buffy faced off with the original Hansel and Gretel, but she was also forced to conquer the Grimm-inspired child-eater Der Kindestod and the The Gentlemen of the dialogue-absent, Emmy-winning episode "Hush." So many fairy and folk tales were successfully woven into the genesis and storytelling of Buffy over the years that it's really impossible to separate the two.

Possibly the most successful weaving of fairy tales into contemporary storytelling is the 2000, ten-hour miniseries *The 10th Kingdom.* Of all the shows on this list (though *Faerie Tale Theatre* was probably truest to the Grimm tales, and the jury is still out on today's *Once Upon a Time*), *The 10th Kingdom* stands out as the best. The series begins in contemporary New York, but the fairy tales are not modernized: The premise is that there are nine kingdoms in the storytelling land of fairy. The real world as we know it, accessible only through a magical mirror portal, is merely the tenth.

Despite its poor ratings, *The 10th Kingdom* did win great reviews and ultimately an Emmy for (if only for Outstanding Main Title Design). It's interesting to wonder how the reception might have differed if this miniseries had premiered today, in a world far more ready to welcome fairy tales with open arms. (There are rumors that a sequel called *House of Wolves* was planned; it would have been great to see the cast together again, but it would also have been hard to stand up against the original.)

Another show in the running for Best Contemporary Fairy Tale has just been made available in the U.S. (thank you, Syfy): *Lost Girl*. Our scholars must set aside the basic Grimm and Andersen stories here and look to the old Celtic tales of the Sidhe. *Lost Girl* is the TV show you've always wanted to see, one based on that mass-market, urban-fantasy adventure series you love (or loathe), with the hot chick with a sword and a tramp stamp on the cover. In *Lost Girl,* there are werewolves and sirens on the police force and dwarves running underground pubs, and every fey who comes of age must choose to ally with the Light Fey or the Dark. The titular heroine, an orphaned succubus named Bo, allies herself with no one, choosing her human friends over strange fey. It's the lovely hero myth and allegory of the outcast that weaves itself through these plots. The heaping spoonful of sex that comes with it may be an example of how to make fantasy shows more palatable for the masses, but as seeing as how that's presented as an integral part of the heroine's lifestyle, it's slightly less gratuitous than, say, an HBO series.

It was good timing that *Lost Girl,* a Canadian series, was given a chance in the U.S. market, right when many gave up on *Grimm*. The concept of *Grimm* is awesome: Police investigation of fairy tale murders and a man with a monster-fighting destiny. But too much exposition—and spooky hand-wavium—weighed the storyline down in the first few episodes like a ten-ton anchor, saved only by the divine comedy of the *Blutbad* Monroe. Excessive amounts of excitement and too little useful information left the watcher as clueless as the character of Nick Burkhardt himself—the original fairy stories may have been tedious at times, but they were not quite so obtuse. But that same monster-of-the-week formula that kept Buffy fans coming back for more has served

Grimm well as the season went on, and it's given the characters a chance to settle into their roles. My hope is that when the writers decide to return to the larger arc, it's a bit less we-made-it-up-as-we-went-along.

The one show that seems to have appeared on the scene and become the belle of the ball from the first episode is the aforementioned *Once Upon a Time*. Unfortunately, ABC is owned by Disney, as anyone who watches *Once Upon a Time* will be constantly reminded. Neither the Grimms' nor Charles Perrault's versions of the Snow White tale had the characters of Pongo or Maleficent, nor did they include subtle nods to the TV show *Lost*. (It's also a little tough to see Jennifer Morrison and not wonder if Hugh Laurie is hiding behind a curtain somewhere.) I tend to agree with Zipes on many of his anti-Disney points, and I do hope this series doesn't fall into the same ridiculous, gumdroppy-sweet, misguided holes as the Snow White films. All this aside, *Once Upon a Time* is a pretty darn successful TV show so far, in both ratings and storytelling execution.

Fairy tales became popular throughout history because they could be passed along via the oral tradition, a benefit in a world where the uneducated masses could not read. These days, those masses mostly *choose* not to read—and turn on their televisions instead. They will find wonder tales on that small screen, and beast tales, and fairy stories of all shapes and sizes, both new and old. But I hope that the popularity of these shows fuels a desire in these audiences to seek out the original tales—be those origins Italian, French, German, Dutch, or other—and experience them firsthand. After all, it's not a retelling if you're hearing it for the first time. And the jokes for those of us in the know are much, much funnier.

ABOUT THE AUTHOR

New York Times bestselling author **Alethea Kontis** is a princess, a goddess, a force of nature, and a mess. She's known for screwing up the alphabet, scolding vampire hunters, turning garden gnomes into mad scientists, and making sense out of fairy tales. Alethea is the co-author of Sherrilyn Kenyon's *Dark-Hunter Companion* and penned the AlphaOops series of picture books. She has done multiple collaborations with Eisner-winning artist J.K. Lee, including *The Wonderland Alphabet* and the illustrated Twitter serial "Diary of a Mad Scientist Garden Gnome." Her debut YA fairy tale novel, *Enchanted,* will be published by HMH (Harcourt Books) in 2012.

Straightforward and Unadorned Adventure: A Conversation with Michael J. Sullivan

JEREMY L. C. JONES

With The Riyria Revelations, Michael J. Sullivan wrote the books he wanted to read: fun adventures about loyalty and friendship. He wrote all six installments of the series before releasing the first through a small press, and he later self-published the rest at six-month intervals. His readership grew steadily, and by the fourth or fifth novel it was clear—in many ways, including financial—that the series was a hit. Lighthearted and rollicking, Sullivan's "buddy tales" are set in a world of betrayal and injustice, relaying the adventures of a thief named Royce Melborn and a mercenary named Hadrian Blackwater.

"Royce and Hadrian form the two sides of my personality," says Sullivan. "Imagine the angel and devil on your shoulders. That's them. Most of the time I am Hadrian, dreaming of being the hero, of achieving something worthwhile. I believe in the inherit goodness of people. If given the chance, they'll rise to the occasion. However, in serious situations, it's Royce that comes out, as we are both very protective of the ones we love. I try to keep him at bay, and Royce can be a difficult person to befriend. You have to prove yourself to him, but once you do, heaven help the person who threatens you. Luckily, I get to be Hadrian most of the time. Even Royce doesn't like to be Royce."

Sullivan's prose, as he says below, is "straightforward and unadorned." His plotting is remarkably consistent over the course of the whole series. He employs traditional fantasy tropes but never takes them too seriously. His world is gritty but never glum, realistic but still wondrous. Perhaps most importantly, his is a world of both humor and hope—the books were written for his daughter first, and general readership second.

In November of 2011, Orbit began releasing The Riyria Revelations over a three-month period as *Theft of Swords, Rise of Empire,* and *Heir of Novron.* Each volume contains two novels. With the exception of some line editing, they scarcely deviate from the originals. Below, Sullivan talks about the Big Three of craft —character, plot, and setting—as well as the arc of his career.

In what ways have your children influenced your writing life?

In many ways you can say that they enabled my writing. When we had our first child, my wife and I decided that one of us should concentrate on raising her. Seeing as how Robin's electrical engineering career made significantly more than my commercial artist work, the logical choice was for me to be the one to stay at home. One of the side benefits was that I had time on my hands while Rebecca napped. Since early childhood I had enjoyed writing, so I used my free time to pursue creating novels as more than just a hobby.

Later, after years of rejections, I had given up on writing. My children had grown up and were now in school, so I had returned to commercial art and started my own advertising agency. My then thirteen-year-old daughter had been having difficulty reading—she's dyslexic—so I decided to write something specifically for her. As she preferred to read stories in book form, rather than typed double-spaced manuscript pages, she prodded me into considering publishing again. The rest, as they say, is history.

What's the fun part of writing fiction for you?

This question suggests that there's a portion that isn't fun, but I've yet to encounter that. So I'll just mention the part I enjoy the most, which is creation. I love inventing things. One of my favorite school assignments had been a sixth grade geography project. I had been given a blank piece of paper and asked to draw a map of an island and inhabit it with whatever I wanted. I drew mountains, rivers, forests, and valleys, then I developed various tribes of people with different traditions and histories. I had a blast, but I think I scared the teacher. She got far more than she had been expecting.

So, yeah, the ability to create worlds and characters and put them into impossible predicaments and seeing how it affects them is pretty darn cool. They say some physicians have god complexes, but as a writer I actually get to play god. Can there be a better job?

Where does a novel usually start for you: image, plot, character, historical event, somewhere else altogether? And how do you develop the novel from there?

Each novel is different. In some cases it might be a single question that begs to be answered, such as, "What would you do with unlimited power?" Other times I may have a character or several that I really enjoy, and I'm just looking for the right setting and predicament to place him into. Creating isn't a science; it's random.

For the most part I'm inspired by a lack of something I want to see or read. That's kind of how I got started with The Riyria Revelations. Because my books have many traditional elements, I've heard some people say they are not new or original. I wish that were true. I would love it if I could go to any bookstore and pick up another series just like it. Only I can't. I know of no other series that is a fun adventure aimed at an adult audience (but not littered with profanity, gruesome violence, and pointless, gratuitous sex) that is easy to read with endearing characters set in a world that is as often pleasant as it is frightening. Rowling's Potter books comes the closest, but those are young-adult. Tolkien comes next, but his aren't nearly as easy to read or as fast-paced. So while the elements in the story are as familiar as a gun in a detective thriller, or poison in a murder mystery, The Riyria Revelations are unique as far as the books I'm familiar with.

Can you talk a little bit about building the world of Elan? Where did you start? How did you develop it?

I probably shouldn't admit this, because in fantasy sometimes the world-building is placed on center stage, but for me I look at this aspect as the least important of the three pillars: character, plot, and setting. That being said: As most fantasy authors do, I have created an extensive background to my world. It actually goes back 8,000 years, but for the most part it is the proverbial iceberg, and only a very small portion is ever exposed.

I'm a lover of history—I read it all the time—so I start by developing the timeline. I'm sure that many readers are tired of worlds with multiple races. But for me, the dynamic is a classic one, and I utilize it: men, dwarves, elves, and goblins. My world has its own creationist mythology, including gods that represent each major race. As is often the case, there have been wars between the various nations. When you start reading the books, you're in a world where men dominate. Elves are akin to Jews in the 1930s. Goblins are a boogieman story told to keep children in line. And dwarves are segregated from one another, lest they gain an upper hand.

But such was not always the case. There was a great war between men and elves, and it was only by the hand of the demigod Novron, the patron of mankind, that men were saved from total elimination by elven-kind. This aspect really is only hinted at in early parts of the book, but it is the entire impetus for the series as a whole. And men and elves eventually conflict again in the final volume, *Percepliquis*.

What part of Elan would you most like to visit?

Why, Percepliquis, of course. This is the ancient capital of the original empire that was destroyed and lost over a thousand years ago. It holds great secrets into mankind's past, including many related to the war (and the end of the impending truce) spoken about above. It represented the height of civilization in the world of Elan. When it fell, much was lost, including magic and the great fighting techniques of the Teshlor. It is the dream of nearly every adventurer in Elan, and it's strictly forbidden to even search for it. I'm a big fan of adventure, for going places where I'm not allowed, so how could I not want to visit there? I'm glad I did eventually get to go and could bring others along with me during its exploration.

And what part would you least like to visit?

There are actually two, and interestingly enough both are prisons: Gutaria and Manzant. Manzant is where one of the main characters, Royce, was imprisoned for years, and it's highly regarded as the foulest place in Elan. Royce is a strong character, hardened by years of betrayal and having to make his way on his own. But even he nearly lost all hope while there. The other prison, Gutaria, is known to only a few, but it is even worse. Built during the time of the original empire, it was constructed with the use of magic. Time does not pass there. What's more, those there are subjected to a dirge that dredges up their worst memory. Luckily for most, it was built to house just a single man, Esrahaddon, the wizard who has been accused of destroying Percepliquis. Having to relive the thing that you want to be forgotten the most, and being forced to endure it forever, seems like a fate worse than death.

Beyond the central characters, Royce and Hadrian, some of the most striking elements of The Riyria Revelations are the series' tone and the style.

I read fiction—and fantasy in particular—for enjoyment rather than for allegories. I feel that the best fantasies are the ones that don't take themselves too seriously, hence the humor that is found in my work. You can, and should, touch on emotional aspects of the human experience and strive to inspire or move people. That's essential to any good writing. But for me, the number-one priority is to entertain, and I write books that I would like to read.

The style of prose I chose for The Riyria Revelations can best be described as straightforward and unadorned. My intention was to make the writing itself invisible to the reader and keep them focused on the characters and plot. In the past, I've written literary fiction where I placed a higher emphasis on the construction of each sentence. Reading that type of novel is like drinking a fine wine. It's meant to be savored and read slowly, enjoying each sip. My hope for that particular piece is that the reader will often pause after a particularly well-crafted sentence. But I feel that style is best suited to stories with simple plots.

The Riyria Revelations, on the other hand, is a very plot-heavy book. A lot happens (it is epic fantasy after all), and my goal was to keep the reader turning pages. I didn't want the prose to get in the way, so I went with a more simplistic style. I wanted the words to fall away and for the events to unfold much like a movie playing in the reader's own imagination. To complete the food analogy, The Riyria Revelations should be like eating popcorn, where there is an unconscious hand-to-mouth motion, until you finally come out of a trance and realize you've just consumed much more than you had intended. I routinely apply this sliding scale between plot and prose complexity on a case-by-case basis. But since few have read my literary fiction, they may not be aware that I actually can utilize both sides of that coin.

As for tone, I wanted it to be light and fun. Sometimes I feel that in pursuit of drama, some writers forget that an important aspect of life is humor. We make jokes when we are happy, when we are nervous, and as a means for coping with fear or pain. Some medieval fantasies seem to take themselves too seriously, as if no one in the Middle Ages ever laughed. I've read books where the world is dark and morbid and filled with morose characters that are unpleasant to be around. I know that the intent is to be more serious or realistic, but for me, this has the opposite effect. I can't help but think, "Okay, no world, no reality, can be this awful for *everyone*." I personally find books with this perspective unpleasant to read. That's not to say that they don't have merit or a deserved fan base. It's just that my preferred tastes run differently.

I was also striving to make the series an easy read, the kind of books that would be appreciated even to people who don't generally read fantasy. For example, my dialogue has an intentionally *modern* style. I didn't want an overly formal or archaic sound, which would stand as an obstacle to readers. Making a movie based in France for an American audience might be more authentic if subtitles were used, but I would find it annoying and distracting. Elan is an invented reality, and I can make people speak anyway I wish. If my goal was to create a sense of otherworldliness, then using archaic or invented language would make sense. But like I said, I wanted to remove all obstacles and let the story flow effortlessly. I should clarify, before some people take me to task, that I do have some invented words. Some of the spellings and pronunciations may seem overly difficult. But I've done that for specific reason in regard to plot. They are not arbitrary decisions.

One last thing I'd like to speak about with regard to style: The books are intended for adult audiences, but I do avoid scenes with sex or overtly graphic violence. This wasn't done because of some kind of moral decision. I just didn't see that adding such things would add to the story. I do like the unintended effect that it makes the books readable by people of varying ages, and I've enjoyed letters from parents that mention they and their children are able to have a shared experience.

How do you go about writing fight scenes?

I hate fight scenes. Not because I am particularly nonviolent, but because they are, oddly enough, boring. Making a fight scene interesting, rather than a series of physical movements, is tough. Every element in a story needs to be a story onto itself. A chapter is a short story; a scene has to have its own story arc. A fight scene needs to be its own mini-drama with a beginning, middle, and an end. This is what makes a fight interesting and memorable.

The role it plays in the narrative can be varied. It can reinforce that the story isn't just fun and games—people die in these books. That fact helps ground the reader and reminds them that there are genuine dangers even though the story is a romp. A good fight scene can also as the payoff for many tension-builds. There are just some times when you really want to see some jerk get what's coming to him.

Why do so many readers leap into the stories at word one and stay there till the end? Why do they keep eating the popcorn?

I think this is a question I should be asking the reader, but since I wrote the story to be tailor-made to my particular tastes, I guess I'll talk a bit about what I was shooting for. When I looked at books that I have enjoyed most over the years, a common thread emerged. They were all good stories about characters I wished I were friends with in real life, which occurred in settings I wanted to actually visit or even live in. A lot of people really like Royce and Hadrian and the banter between them. They recognize a deep sense of loyalty between the two, and I think they would like to be a part of that.

One of the things I wanted to do is provide an escape into a place that is better than reality. One of my favorite TV shows is *The West Wing*. It may not be an *accurate* portrayal of what working at the White House would be like, but it showed a world that I *wanted* it to be. Especially in the early seasons where everyone was depicted as intelligent, hard-working, and striving to make a difference. I would have liked to have been a part of that and surrounded by those characters.

That's not to say that I write worlds that are all sunshine and rainbows. Sure my books have serious moments, dark moments—you have to have these to create tension. There has to be a low point to provide contrast for joy. My characters have not led ideal lives, and I place many challenges before them. But through it all there is a current of optimism that runs through the stories. I think people enjoy being a part of their triumphs. Perhaps people stay glued because they really care about the characters and want to see what will happen to them.

One other element that I've heard is a big draw for people: Each of the six books has its own self-contained conflict and resolution, but it exists within a framework where there is an overarching story with mysteries that unfold a bit at a time. This could only be accomplished because I wrote the whole series before publishing the first book. I often would go back to an early novel and add a scene or two to further enhance a plot point that was occurring late in the story arc. Many books provide all you ever need to know about the world and the characters in the first book, and the rest are just "more of the same." Because I had the freedom to work with a larger canvas, I could reveal the history of the world and the backstories of the characters a little at a time. There are things that I only initially hint at that eventually come to light. So I think a lot of people are seeking to find that next puzzle piece and see how it fits in place.

What makes for a compelling protagonist in general and a compelling fantasy protagonist in particular?

I don't really see that genre has much to do with compelling characters. There are certain things that are universal, regardless of genre. Myron is often cited as a favorite in the series even though he has very little time on stage. For those that are early in the series: Yes, he comes back, but not until the last two books. I need to use my big guns sparingly. When I saw the movie *WALL-E,* I thought, "They stole Myron!": unassuming, kind-hearted, and optimistic beyond reason. I think the single most important aspect of a likeable character is one that doesn't whine. No matter how awful things get, they just don't complain.

I also think people respect characters that take responsibility for their own actions—or for that matter even act at all. Likeable characters don't sit on the sidelines and expect someone else to do what needs doing. They are men and women of action. If you want to make them even more sympathetic, place them in situations where *they* know they don't stand a chance. Their deeds are further amplified if accompanied by people who remind them that they aren't expected, or even supposed, to do anything that is not in their own self-interest.

What about an antagonist?

Antagonists are actually easy—much easier. You just have to put someone at odds against the protagonist, but give him a good reason for doing so. I find it works well to portray a protagonist as a determined individual with a very reasonable goal (sometimes even a noble goal). The problem arises because these people are short-sighted and pursue their desires regardless of the costs. They are the ones that console themselves with the notion that the ends justify the means.

It's easier for people to be accepting of antagonists, as there are so many in the real world to use as examples. Heroes are rare, which is why people like reading about them. Most antagonists, while not evil, are often self-centered, misguided, and unsympathetic to others. No one ever thinks of himself as evil or bad. We all think we are the good guys. So an antagonist, in order to be believable, has to feel this way too, and be recognized by those around him as trying to do good. Being evil for evil sake is as unrealistic as a lack of humor.

Did you do much editing of the original tales in preparation for the Orbit editions? If so, did the chance to go back over them reveal anything to you about yourself and your writing? About the characters or the world?

Nothing frightened me more than getting back the changes from the editor. I had created a very intricately woven plot, and pulling on one thread could unravel an entire tapestry. I also constructed my series in an unusual way—that is, different than how most stories are created. I'm speaking about the timing of how I expose details about my characters and the world. To get published is so difficult. The first book has to be strong—really, really strong—and there is often a lot of front-loading, giving enough meat for the readers to really sink their teeth into. When I wrote the books, I had no intention on publishing. I doled out details slowly, over the course of the entire series. My audience had been myself, my family, and friends. I knew they would read the whole thing. But for someone else, they may find the first books lacking in detail and conclude it is because of poor writing skill—when in fact it was by design.

In any case, I thought that to make the books "marketable," they might need major rework. What if Orbit had declared that "buddy tales" weren't popular and wanted to make either Royce or Hadrian a woman? What if they wanted to add a love interest? What if they needed more revealed earlier in the stories? Any changes like those would have been a huge problem, and I'm not sure that I would have been willing to make such concessions.

Luckily my concerns turned out to be unfounded. Orbit loved the books just as they were, and they realized that the plot was already very sound. They didn't find any holes that needed plugging (thanks to my wife Robin who had already taken care of them when they were originally published). Their only problem was that the book didn't start with Royce and Hadrian; I had started the book with two minor characters, Archibald and Victor. Others who had read the series had had the same reaction, so it made perfect sense to change. For those that have read the original version, and who want to read the new opening, they can read the free sample of *Theft of Swords* from my blog (www.riyria.com). It's there in its entirety. That really was the only major change.

The biggest revelation that the process unveiled was that I wasn't completely delusional about the strength of the story as originally written. A lot of my insecurities had been alleviated by the high sales and positive reviews when they were originally self-published, but it felt good to know that professionals in the industry appreciated what I had written. On the technical side, I did learn a great deal by reviewing the numerous changes from the line editors, although I'll probably always struggle with the placement of commas. Orbit has a great team of very detail-oriented copyeditors and proofreaders. I was constantly amazed at the things they found and embarrassed by some of the mistakes that were still present—even after more than a half dozen editors had worked on the books over the years.

From the time you penned your first Royce and Hadrian tale to the most recent, has much changed for you? Professionally and in terms of craft?

Having come from the "indie" world, a lot has changed for me in regards to income. When I started, and for several years after, I made little more than enough to pay for an occasional dinner out, assuming we didn't buy any wine. It wasn't until my fourth book was released that my income started paying some of the bills. And on the fifth book, I started making enough to match my wife's income. Even before the series was bought by Orbit, I had graduated to earning enough money to be self-supporting, which I consider quite an accomplishment, since there are many traditionally published authors (some with multiple book releases) who haven't reached that milestone yet and have to keep their day jobs to pay for bills or insurance.

My goals have definitely changed. When I started The Riyria Revelations, I had no intention on publishing. But now, one of my main goals is to continue to be able to write full-time. Whether I'll be successful at that, it's hard to say. Income can be so sporadic. Most writers don't earn out their advances, and you get those payments only at major milestones. It can be months or even years between checks. I had socked away a lot of the money that I made from self-publishing, and I'm being cautious about spending the money made from the Orbit and foreign translations. I feel like I'm in a race to see what line is crossed first: depletion of my nest egg or the next book's release. Still, I can't complain. While I would hate for the financial freedom to be just a brief respite, it's more than many authors will ever see, and I consider myself fortunate to have done it for any length of time.

As to the craft of writing, a great deal has changed. He who does not evolve dies, or at least he should. I'm always working on becoming a better writer. While it's true that my entire series was written at once, the books still took me four and a half years. From what I can see, my voice and style has definitely improved over time. I hope I never get to a stage with my writing where I become too arrogant or inflexible not to continue to push for constant, incremental improvement. I do believe that writing is a craft, and it takes years to move from apprentice to master. Where on the scale am I? I'm not sure, but it's a muscle that I'll continue to strengthen the more I use it.

As to professionally, I guess the first thing that has changed is this: I now feel like I can say that I have one—a profession, that is. When you self-publish, even if you make significant money, there is still doubt in the back of your mind whether you'll be chastised for applying the label "professional writer" to yourself. There is no doubt that I'm taken much more seriously now that I have the traditional stamp of approval. It's manifested in all kinds of ways: requests to blurb other authors' books, speaking engagement requests (I recently did a talk at the Library of Congress), the way my online interactions are taken, and requests from people to do interviews. When I was self-published, I always felt like I was standing with downcast eyes and my hat in hand when talking about my books. Nowadays I feel that I'm *allowed* to speak about them with my head held high, and that removes a lot of stress.

What's next for you?

Going back to the last question, the only way to guarantee steady income is to keep writing. Since finishing the edits for The Riyria Revelations in June of 2011, I've been busy working on my next books. I have three written, and I'm about fifty-percent done with a fourth. Of course, I'm hoping that Orbit will pick them up as well, but I've not submitted anything . . . *yet*. The next project that will likely hit the street will be *Antithesis*: Two opposing individuals possess limitless magic, providing the universe balance. An unexpected death transfers this power to an unsuspecting bystander who is clueless of the consequences of his newfound abilities.

I tend to write my own "back of the book blurbs" or "elevator speech" and do so early on to help me articulate what a book is about. This is what I have so far:

Have you ever wondered how the world will end?

No? Well, don't sweat it. Most people don't, and the few that do expect the cause will be a dramatic change in climate, a pandemic, or mostly likely war. That's what we've all been taught to believe, and we're comfortable with rational explanations. But people weren't always so quick to accept the facts provided by so-called experts. There used to be a time when we believed in myth and magic. Our minds were open to the idea of things that couldn't be seen . . . the fantastical.

Having been that way myself, I can understand the propensity . . . but then I met Winston Stewart and learned to believe that there are other forces at work—not the least of which is fate. Fate is an amazing thing. It put Gandhi in South Africa, Nelson at Gibraltar, and Winston Stewart on that train in Alexandria, Virginia.

You don't know who Winston Stewart is? You will.

I'm also keeping my ear to the ground about how The Riyria Revelations are being received and whether people want more. There are many ideas I have for prequels—or even sequels set in the far distant future. What I won't do is tack on to Percepliquis, the last book. The series was carefully choreographed to end as it did. To extend directly to that story would ruin something that I feel is pretty special as it is. But Riyria existed for twelve years before the start of _The Crown Conspiracy,_ and Royce and Hadrian had many exciting escapades that could be explored. Also, I could do a series of books about the original empire and the fall of Percepliquis, or go even further back in time to the original war between men and elves. I really like the idea that the religious beliefs that Elan holds in the days of The Riyria Revelations are actually myths that have been distorted over time. The "actual" events would have been much different than what they have been led to believe.

So I'm watching and waiting. I'm very conscious of not "milking the series." I'm really happy with what I created, and I don't want to be like one of those television series that stays around long past its prime. I think there are two ingredients that are required: first, have a compelling story to tell, and secondly, have an audience interested in reading it. I think I have plenty of the first, but I'm going to let the readers decide if there are any of the second. To that end, I do have a work-in-progress area of my blog where people can vote on which stories they would be most interested in. Bottom line: I don't want to overstay my welcome in Elan. But if people want more, I'm more than happy to oblige.

Any parting words of advice, encouragement, or mischief?

Many readers of fantasy also feel like they have a book inside waiting to get out. To them I say, "Go for it." Even if you write something only for your own enjoyment, you never know where that may take you.

As for life in general: I'm glad that I learned early on that life is too short to do something you don't enjoy doing. I'm fortunate to have a wife that was willing to support me while I chased, and eventually caught, my dream. Without getting too *Princess Bride* on you, I do believe in true love, and if you can find yours, your life will always be spectacular.

As for mischief: I'm a rebel. I believe in doing things my way. I don't mind bucking a system (or two or three). Know that you can be in complete control of your own life, if you only dare to step off the well-worn path. And last but not least, live by the immortal words of the classically trained and revered philosophers of *Galaxy Quest:* "Never give up! Never surrender!"

ABOUT THE AUTHOR

Jeremy L. C. Jones is a freelance writer, editor, and teacher. He is the Staff Interviewer for *Clarkesworld Magazine* and a frequent contributor to *Kobold Quarterly* and *Booklifenow.com*. He teaches at Wofford College and Montessori Academy in Spartanburg, SC. He is also the director of Shared Worlds, a creative writing and world-building camp for teenagers that he and Jeff VanderMeer designed in 2006. Jones lives in Upstate South Carolina with his wife, daughter, and flying poodle.

Another Word: Dear Speculative Fiction, I'm Glad We Had This Talk
ELIZABETH BEAR

Look.

I'm sitting down to have this conversation with you as a friend, as somebody who loves you. As somebody who's devoted thirty-odd years of her life to you.

We've all made some mistakes. We've all had moments in our lives when we got a little self-important, maybe. Where our senses of humor failed us.

I'm as guilty as anyone of taking myself too seriously.

But for you, it's become an addiction. You seem to think that nothing fun can have value; that only grimdark portentousness and dystopia mean anything. You wallow in human suffering and despair, and frankly—it makes me tired.

I remember when we were younger. You were so clever, so playful. So much fun. We had some good times. You could make me laugh and think at the same time. You made my pulse race.

But we got older and started understanding a little better how complicated the world is. How layered people's motivations are. At first, you seemed to handle the moral complexity well. You'd give me something like *The Forever War* or *The Left Hand of Darkness*, and we could talk about it for hours.

I mean, I sensed your ambivalence. But I had some ambivalence of my own. That's the thing about ambivalence—it's a kind of tension. And tension drives a narrative, right?

And I don't know if you got uncomfortable with the tension? Maybe you felt like you couldn't live in limbo anymore, but you'd seen too much to believe in happy endings anymore. I'm guessing, I admit—but I wonder if you felt like had to find some way to resolve things. Get some closure. And escapism . . . just wasn't open to you any more.

You started thinking you had to be cynical and mean to accomplish anything. You got wrapped up in your own history and your long-running arguments. You buried yourself in the seriousness of it all, and you forgot how to tell a joke. You even got—I hate to say it—kind of pretentious. Didactic, even.

The thing is, that kind of cynical pose is really just a juvenile reaction to the world not being what we hoped. We can't have everything—so we reject anything. But it's adolescent, darling, and most of us outgrow it. We realize that as much as the world can be a ball of dung, and horrible things can happen for no reason, there are positive outcomes too, sometimes. I'm not going to say things balance out, because of course they don't—life is not fair—but it's not just awful, either.

I'm not crying out for slapstick, here. You know that's never done it for me. And I'm certainly not saying that I want you to be shallower.

If anything, I'm asking you to be deeper—to embrace more of the range of human experience. Not just the bad times. I mean, sure, we need to acknowledge the bad times, and I've deeply admired your recent willingness to explore new perspectives, to take on issues of race and gender and sexuality that once you would have shied from.

I have never doubted your courage.

But look at Terry Pratchett. (I know, we should all be Terry Pratchett. But then what would *he* read?) He manages to be incisive without being pretentious. He manages to be sharp and illuminating *by* being funny. Look at Neil Gaiman. Here's a guy who can tackle some hard subjects and still have a good time. He makes people like him, and because they like him, they listen when he says hard, important things.

I almost hate to bring it up, but . . . J.K. Rowling? I know, you don't take her seriously. She's a woman, and she writes for kids, and in fairness some of the later books . . . could have used a closer encounter with the blue pencil. So it's easy for you to dismiss her. But what you can't dismiss is that she reaches people—and whether you agree with the way she discusses issues like class bigotry or not, the fact is, she does discuss them. Her awareness of them saturates her work, and it gets into people's heads—because millions of people *read* her work.

I guess what I'm saying here is, look at Lenny Bruce. Look at George Carlin. The angrier they got, the less fun they got—and the less effective they got, because nobody wants to listen to an old man cat-yell at the kids on his lawn.

Oh, honey, I'm not saying you're old. And I'm not leaving you. You're a big part of my life, and I will always be here for you. I'm just trying to make sure that you're always here for *me*, and sitting there in a toxic stew of your own bitterness . . . it's not good for you. *Look at you.* When was the last time you left the house? When was the last time you read something because it was *fun*, not because you thought it was good for you?

Stern-lipped moral uprightness is not a literary value, darling. Sure, theme is. I'm not disputing that. But did you know that John Gardner talked about this thing he called "disPollyanna Syndrome?" He considered it a literary vice—the cynical fallacy that the real world is unrelievedly bleak—and he considered it as great a disservice to art as its opposite. And . . . he cited Harlan Ellison as a chief practitioner in this mode.

Oh, I heard you gasp. But the New Wave is one of the primary influences on the way we live our life and do our work today. And also, I hear you say, Harlan was popular! And funny!

Well, yes, he was funny. That's why he got away with it. But you? I feel like all we have anymore is pus and severed limbs and the eschaton. And that's not something we can build a future on, is it?

Kind of by definition.

I'm just saying that it's right—and humane and morally correct—to harbor a deep and abiding concern for the world around you. And that it's a perfectly normal—even laudable!—trait to express that concern and draw attention to problems by being savagely trenchant, witty, and sarcastic. Caustic, even. I want you to speak out. I want you to say what you mean.

But sometimes lately, spending time with you is like having my face pressed down into a trough of human misery until the bubbles stop.

You can have a sense of humor too. It's *okay*. We'll *still like you*. We'll still take you seriously. We just think it'd be best for all of us if you could let yourself unbend just a little.

I know. It's easier to get people to take you seriously when you're all grit and pus and urban decay—or all gut wounds and bureaucratic incompetence, for that matter. It seems like a quick route to street cred. But the thing is, real people generally aren't miserable all the time. Even in horrible situations, they find ways to take a little pleasure, to crack jokes. Dying people and homicide cops and soldiers are generally really funny.

I want us to have a little pleasure again too.

And maybe we'd have more friends if you weren't such a downer to be around all the time.

ABOUT THE AUTHOR

Elizabeth Bear was born on the same day as Frodo and Bilbo Baggins, but in a different year. This, coupled with a childhood tendency to read the dictionary for fun, led her inevitably to penury, intransigence, the mispronunciation of common English words, and the writing of speculative fiction. She has published nearly a hundred short stories and twenty novels, the most recent of which is *Range of Ghosts* from Tor (2012). Among her genre honors are two Hugo Awards and a Sturgeon Award. She grew up in New England and lived in Las Vegas for seven years. She now resides in central Massachusetts, where she shares half of an eleventy-two-year-old house with a giant ridiculous dog. She has no plans to leave the Northeast ever again, except on brief exploratory excursionsand regular visits to western Wisconsin, the domicile of her partner, notorious (and brilliant) fantasist, Scott Lynch.

From the Editor's Desk
NEIL CLARKE

I don't enjoy writing editorials. I much prefer to be behind the scenes, picking stories or artwork, but this month I feel obligated to say something. As you may have heard, last month, I was nominated for a Hugo Award in the Best Editor Short Form category. It blew my mind. Since *Clarkesworld* is my only editing job, this nomination can only come from you, our readers. I'm very overwhelmed by your support. Thank you! The honor is even more special to me as it is the first time an editor has been nominated purely on the basis of work done in a digital medium. As someone remembers when online fiction was considered second-class, this means a lot to me.

Clarkesworld is also represented in the Hugos by the fiction of E. Lily Yu (Best Short Story Nominee, "The Cartographer Wasps and the Anarchist Bees", April 2011) and Catherynne M. Valente (Best Novella Nominee, "Silently and Very Fast", Nov-Dec. 2011). Furthermore, two articles originally published in *Clarkesworld* appear in Daniel M. Kimmel's Best Related Work-nominated book, *Jar Jar Binks Must Die . . . and Other Observations about Science Fiction Movies*. While not officially a Hugo, the Campbell Award for Best New Writer is part of the Hugo ceremony. This year, we are very pleased to see E. Lily Yu among the list of very talented Campbell nominees. Our congratulations and best wishes go to all of them.

The Hugo's weren't the only good news for Catherynne M. Valente. She's just sold two novels to Tor, one of which is based on "The Radiant Car Thy Sparrows Drew" from *Clarkesworld* #35. Can't wait for that one!

While I might not enjoy editorials, they are something I need to work on. Last month, I used our social networking presence on Twitter and Facebook to solicit some ideas for future editorials. The suggestions were all over the map, but a few homed in on the changes we've gone through over the years and data we've collected in regards to reading, writing and online fiction. That seems like a good theme to cover in our fifth anniversary year. Have you ever been curious about our readership, most popular stories, the slush pile or the trends we've observed? Now's your chance to ask. Email me at neil@clarkesworldmagazine.com or leave a comment on our website and I'll try to work those angles into next month's issue.

Until next time, thanks for reading!

-Neil

ABOUT THE AUTHOR

Neil Clarke is the editor of *Clarkesworld Magazine,* owner of Wyrm Publishing and a 2012 Hugo Nominee for Best Editor (short form). He currently lives in NJ with his wife and two children.

ABOUT THE ARTIST
JESSADA SUTTHI

Jessada Sutthi a concept artist with five years experience in the entertainment industry. He has done freelance work for games, book covers and card games in addition to providing matte painting and concept arts for various animated works and TV advertisements. He currently works for Studio Hive, originally joining the staff as senior concept artist. He was promoted to Art Director in 2012.

WEBSITE

jessada-art.deviantart.com

15107684R00039

Made in the USA
Charleston, SC
18 October 2012